# MISSING!

"Let's all be sensible," said the man. "We don't want anyone getting hurt, do we?"

What did he mean, be sensible? How would I get hurt? He was horrible. Anyone who wore dark glasses in the rain had to be hiding something.

When Joanne's stepfather mysteriously disappears she doesn't know where to turn for help. The police don't seem to be interested, her mother is abroad and there's something sinister about the man looking after her neighbour Peter. In desperation Joanne tells her Scottish friends Neil and Roddy. But how can they help?

JANICE BROWN lives with her husband and three children in Scotland. A former teacher, she now divides her time between writing, bringing up the family and her favourite pastime of listening to music.

For Gyda, Paul and Kathryn

# MISSING!

## Janice Brown

A LION PAPERBACK

Oxford · Batavia · Sydney

Copyright © 1990 Janice Brown

Published by
**Lion Publishing plc**
Sandy Lane West, Oxford, England
ISBN 0 7459 1876 X
**Lion Publishing Corporation**
1705 Hubbard Avenue, Batavia, Illinois 60510, USA
ISBN 0 7459 1876 X
**Albatross Books Pty Ltd**
PO Box 320, Sutherland, NSW 2232, Australia
ISBN 0 7324 0211 5

First edition 1990

*The characters and situations in this book are entirely imaginary
and bear no relation to any real person or actual happening.*

**British Library Cataloguing in Publication Data**
Brown, Janice
　Missing!
　I. Title
　823'.914 [F]
　ISBN 0 7459 1876 X

**Library of Congress Cataloging in Publication Data**
Brown, Janice.
　　Missing! / Janice Brown. — 1st ed.
　　　　p.　cm. — (A Lion paperback)
　　ISBN 0 7459 1876 X
　　[1. Mystery and detective stories.　2. Kidnapping—Fiction.]
　I. Title.
　PZ7.B81419Mi　1990
　[Fic]—dc20

Printed and bound in Great Britain
by Cox & Wyman Ltd, Reading

# CONTENTS

# PROLOGUE
# Sardines for Christmas

"Another one for you," my stepfather said, handing me a small rectangular package.

Ten layers of tissue paper later, what emerged was a tin of sardines. The silliest Christmas present I'd ever had, but somehow one of the best. Not that Brian or Mum would ever understand why.

It was from a boy called Neil Campbell. He was the son of an old art-school friend of my mother who lived on a Scottish island. I'd spent the previous summer with the Campbells while Brian and my mother had honeymooned in Italy. Brian had never met any of them, and I had the feeling he thought they were a bit strange. I'd thought that at first myself. In fact, I'd begun by hating Neil and his twin brother, Roddy, although I'd ended up liking them a lot.

I looked again at the present Roddy had sent, which I'd opened first, a few minutes earlier. It was a framed black-and-white photograph of their house, with traces of snow melting on the roof, the loch glinting and black behind it, and snow-capped hills beyond. Although it was a winter picture, it brought back vivid memories of the summer.

Neil's tin of sardines was, I knew, his idiotic way of

doing the same thing. It was meant to remind me of the day when he'd dropped a wet trout on my bare feet as I was sunbathing by the loch.

He was an idiot. Funny, restless, quick-tempered like me, but loyal and dependable too. Bespectacled Roddy was quieter, more easygoing, more thoughtful, but he could be funny as well. It hurt me to think of them and remember the good times we'd had. I put the photograph aside. It didn't seem likely I'd see them this summer. Mum and Mrs Campbell had been exchanging letters, and there was a chance they'd be using our house for a holiday while we were away. Brian was taking us to Cornwall to see the haunts of his childhood.

"They are quite normal, these friends of yours?" I heard him ask Mum as I unwrapped the sardines.

"I expect it's some kind of Scottish custom. Like haggis. They'll probably leave us a haggis if they come in the summer," she smiled brightly.

"I don't object to them using our house, Anne, but I positively draw the line at eating haggis," Brian frowned.

Then he picked up the present Mr and Mrs Campbell had sent me, a small, red leather book of verses from the Bible, one page for each day of the year. I meant to use it but, from the look on Brian's face, I could tell he thought it was just as strange a present as the sardines, so I kept my mouth shut. He flicked through the pages, then smiled, saying something about "Chairman Mao's little red book".

Mum laughed, then said, "Before your time, Joanne."

They went out together to make some coffee. I went to the window and leaned on the sill. Outside, the dry beech leaves on the hedge shifted in the wind. Beyond the garden, empty fields stretched towards the village

8

a mile away. I heard Mum laugh in the kitchen, and I sighed.

These days so many things were "before my time". "In"-jokes, little things they would say that left me feeling vaguely stupid, unsure whether to smile or not. Maybe that was why my thoughts went back so often to the summer.

Out of curiosity, I looked up the verse on the page for 25 December: "There is wonderful joy ahead even though the going is rough for a while down here."

I thought about how life had changed since Mum married Brian. The second bit of the verse was right. I wasn't so sure about the first part.

# 1
# Try to look happy

Winter passed and spring came, and the going didn't get any easier. One particular night was tougher than most.

We were in the car, ready to drive away, when Brian half-turned, as if seeing me for the first time.

"Why isn't she wearing a dress?"

Mum twisted round to look at me.

"Why aren't you wearing a dress, dear?"

"Because I don't *have* any dresses," I said.

"Wonderful," Brian's jaw set in annoyance. He thrust the car into gear and we were off.

I heard him mutter ". . . wore a dress at the wedding last year, didn't she?"

Mum explained patiently that it had been hired.

From what I could see of his face in the driver's mirror, I had the feeling he wished I'd been hired too. And returned to the shop.

What did it matter if I was wearing trousers? If Brian wanted to show off his newly-acquired wife and stepdaughter, his colleagues and their wives would have to like me in trousers or leave me.

They left me. At the house I did the wrong thing at the very start. I sat down. Sitting down in a room full of standing strangers is a big mistake. I didn't have the courage to stand up again. Clutching my fizzy apple juice, I tried to look happy. But I clashed with the room and the room was winning.

Dusky pink curtains, soft grey carpet, polished parquet, antique china plates on floral wallpaper, a faint scent of polish overlaid right now with expensive perfume, aftershave and cigarette smoke: it all breathed good breeding and gentility. I didn't stand a chance.

Even Mum had forsaken me. She was by the window, talking to a large-nosed lady in blue. She looked gorgeous in her white shirt-waister and jade green jacket, her dark red hair up in an elegant French pleat. But could she really be enjoying all this? It was so phoney. These women hardly knew one another. They had nothing in common except husbands working in the same law firm.

Was this really my mother, my calm, patient, lovely mother, usually so absorbed in her paintings that she forgot to eat? Mostly she didn't care what she was wearing either. Tonight she looked like a stranger. A Lawyer's Wife. How well did I know her? Could you actually live with someone for fifteen years, and end up not knowing them? Or had these ten months changed her into someone else?

A plate with tiny cheesy biscuits on it was thrust at me out of the noise. I was starving. How many was it polite to take? Five? Ten? I took two, and the second one flaked all over my trousers.

The cause of all my woe was standing in a cluster of men next to the fireplace, legs apart, one hand in trouser pocket, the other wrapped round a glass. Smiling. Immaculate to the last gold cuff-link. He said something, and they all laughed. Everybody thought Brian was wonderful.

To be fair, if he'd been my uncle, I might have

11

thought he was moderately wonderful too. Some days I almost did. Then I'd find myself almost hating him. I couldn't get my feelings straightened out at all. I'd had nearly a year to get used to him and I could as easily have got used to a wart on the tip of my nose.

He and Mum were happy. I had to admit that. But I wasn't happy. Sometimes I felt like a canvas with one portrait on the surface and the real one hidden under layers of paint. It wasn't any way to live.

"*So* glad you were able to come," a large lady interrupted my thoughts. On she warbled, not waiting for me to speak. ". . . so lovely to meet Brian's two lovely ladies at last. And do you like living in the country? So *clever* of Brian to find a house so quickly. Typical of him. Simply *must* let us all come to admire it . . ."

*Who is she?* I wondered desperately. Her lower lip mesmerised me. It turned out curiously when she spoke, so that you saw clearly the line where her bright lipstick ended and the dull red of her lip began. She "Joanne'd" me in every sentence, as if she'd read that good conversation depended on it. At last I remembered. She was our hostess, Pamela. And she was doing her hostess number on me.

"Forgive me, dear, did Brian say you were at college?"

"No, I'm still at school. I'm hoping to go to art school. I'd like to go to St Martin's. If I'm good enough."

"How lovely."

I could sense her adjusting to talk to a school girl.

"Well, I'm sure you'll do nicely . . ."

She beamed at me. Her lip did its funny quiver again.

What did she mean, "do nicely"? How did an artist "do nicely"? I stared blankly at her.

Still beaming, she excused herself. It was time to supervise the food.

I felt like begging the keys from Mum and sitting in the car for the rest of the evening. These people knew nothing about the things that mattered. Painting would never be something I did "nicely", just to earn a living. I didn't want to "do nicely". I wanted to do brilliantly. I wanted to astonish people with the genius of my paintings. Talking to Pamela left me feeling drained and squashed like a flattened Coke can.

Reluctantly I followed the drift to the dining-room. We shuffled round a table of salads and meats, dips and rice, pastas in strange sauces, breads and patés. A balding man wearing a bow tie tried to fill my glass with wine.

"You won't persuade her, George. She's a lady of independent mind," Brian's voice cut through my awkward refusing.

"Show me the woman who isn't, old son," the bald man laughed, turning away in search of more glasses. Brian and I were left facing one another, a small desert of silence in the noise.

He pointed at a corner of my plate.

"What's that?"

"Saffron rice with prawns."

He scooped a little off my plate, and eyed it for a moment.

"I'm allergic to something. Don't think it's prawns. However, if I fall down foaming at the mouth in the next twenty seconds, you'll be able to tell them it wasn't the butler."

It was meant to be a joke. I smiled.

"You're surviving, are you? So far?"

"I'm all right."

"Good."

Did he mean it? Was he really bothered whether I was miserable or not? He drained his wine glass. I wondered how much he'd already had. Maybe the wine was making him nice to me.

"What's the matter?"

I felt embarrassed, as if my thoughts were suddenly visible on my forehead like those flickering adverts in supermarkets.

"Don't worry," he said, smiling. "I may be a lost soul, but I'm not an alcoholic yet." He glanced from the empty glass to me again. "Your mother's driving tonight, if that's what's bothering you."

I bent my head to the prawns, feeling my face flush. I was all muddled up. Around us, the conversations were getting louder and sillier. I didn't like the idea that he might drink too much, because I didn't want to see him look silly. But he annoyed me too. I knew he didn't take my faith seriously, but he didn't need to make a joke of it. Anyway, he was wrong if he thought I wasn't drinking wine because of what I believed. I just didn't like the taste. We'd rarely had wine at home before Mum had married Brian. Mum had always said she'd rather spend what money we had on other things.

"So this is the little one, eh?"

"Joanne, this is Jackson Taylor."

He was a smallish, dark-haired man in shirt-sleeves.

"Entranced to meet you, Joanne. I'm sure you've heard nothing but good of me. Still on the first course? I've gone straight for this delicious raspberry stuff."

I mumbled politely. Brian had never mentioned him. From his expression, he didn't seem desperately enthusiastic about him now either.

". . . not that you can believe a word this fellow tells you," a spoonful of raspberries waved in Brian's

14

direction. "Which *I* dare to say who shouldn't, since he *is* my boss. Mind you, Joanne," he put a rather warm hand on my shoulder, "mind you, I have nothing but admiration for him. Takes on cases where the rest of us fear to tread, like the lovely Mrs Delaney, for example. Now there's one that sorts the men from the boys . . ."

The hand on my shoulder felt clammy through my shirt, like a giant slug.

"Go and bore someone else, Jackson."

Jackson's jaw dropped. Brian said it again.

The hand lifted from my shoulder. With an attempt at a joke he turned towards the table. I wanted the carpet to open and swallow me. How could Brian be so rude?

A man with a red bow tie appeared and began talking to him. I edged away. My face felt like a hot red balloon. I went back to the room we'd started from and, to my relief, Mum was there already, with a small group of wives. There was a space next to her on the sofa.

"Tired?" she asked.

I shrugged my shoulders.

"We'll be going soon," she said, reassuringly.

Soon seemed to take forever. I closed my eyes. Voices, voices, voices. Would they never weary? The men had drawn into a close group next door in the dining-room. Raucous male laughter spilled out, receded, then spilled like waves again towards our little chintz island of gentility.

I opened my eyes. A thin woman with huge glasses and dangly silver ear-rings like willow leaves was speaking to me.

"I was just telling Anne," she tinkled her brace-let at Mum. "When you're in Paris you must go to a super boutique in the Rue Lafitte. Cassie and I found it last April. Half the price they charge in London."

"Well, we're really going there to work. Both of us," Mum took my hand and squeezed it. "But if we have time . . ."

"Oh, *make* time, darling." The silver leaves shook at us. "Especially since you're leaving Brian behind. I promise you, the shoes are out of this world."

Pamela appeared in the doorway, looking tired.

"I can't get the men to join us," she said, holding the coffee pot out to us sadly, like a consolation prize. "Not that we're missing anything," she sighed, looking at Silver Ear-rings. "George is telling Jeremy what to do about your drains."

"Spare me the details," Silver Ear-rings raised her hands in mock horror. "Anne, dear," she turned to my mother, "you don't do interior design, do you? I could live with the drains if we could do something about the bathroom. Honestly, I don't think it's been touched since the animals left the ark."

Mum said one of the things she'd liked about our new house was that so little needed doing to it.

"Where are you exactly?" Pamela asked.

Mum told her. Then a woman in a green dress said abruptly, "Isn't that where Carl Niemenen lives?"

Everyone looked at her in surprise. What I know about classical music could be written on the back of a bus ticket, but even *I* had heard of Carl Niemenen.

"I'm sure that's where he lives," she went on, "*The Sunday Times* did a thing on him last year. Or *The Observer*. One of them anyway."

"How thrilling for you, Anne darling," Pamela's mouth did its little turning movements. "He's so incredibly good-looking! All we have round here is a very dull member of the European Parliament."

"I don't imagine he's ever home," Mum commented. "These famous conductors spend their lives flying from one orchestra to the next."

Silver Ear-rings said she wouldn't mind flying the world with him for a month or two, and Pamela shrieked with laughter.

At long last, it was time for home. I waited in the car while Mum and Brian said their good-nights.

The window was down. Two figures came to the car next to ours, their words carrying in the clear night air.

". . . very clever, I should say, but the child is quite sullen."

It was Silver Ear-rings. Her husband grunted something, fiddling with the passenger door lock. Her voice grew high and indignant. "I am *not* being petty, Jeremy."

His answer was too low for me to catch.

"Brian? Don't be naïve, Jeremy. A year, two at the most, you wait and see."

The doors slammed and they drove away. I waited for Mum and Brian, watching the leaves of the laurel bush beside me move lightly in the faint breeze, trying not to think.

They finally appeared. Mum got into the driver's seat.

"All right?" she said to me, before pulling out. "All strapped in, dear?"

From where I sat I could see her face in the driver's mirror. Love for her lodged in my throat like a plum stone and made me dumb. Whatever I thought of Brian, I knew she loved him. I closed my eyes, and closed my mind against the possibility that anything could alter that.

# 2

# Hurt and crumpled

"Good grief, is that blood?"

My step-father's secretary froze, horrified, as she passed me a cup of tea through the hatch.

I looked at my hands, spotted with alizarin crimson.

"We've been painting backcloths for the concert."

Chloe laughed. She was black and beautiful, with the kind of smile they use for toothpaste ads.

"I don't suppose you've done any work at all this week. And you're off to France soon, and Cornwall too? Unfair."

I smiled back at her.

She made a face at me. "We're running round in circles in here. Miss Miller keeps threatening to have migraines." She whispered the last bit, rolling her dark eyes as if she was going crazy.

Miss Miller was Brian's cashier. She had her own small room on the far side of the secretaries' room, and ruled them like a tyrant. There were three of them — Chloe, Mary, a quiet fair-haired girl, and Joyce, who was stout and wore spectacles on a chain.

Miss Miller had frightened me at first, but now I was used to her. Besides, as Mr Barnes-Ingram's daughter, I could do no wrong. She had worked for the firm when Brian's father had been alive.

"He's nearly finished," Chloe told me. "Would you like a biscuit with that?"

I said no, and she slid back the glass with a friendly wink.

I'd drunk most of my tea when the outer door swung open. A dark-haired woman strode in. She had a wicker basket with some packages in it, and she was wearing a bright red suit. Instantly I thought — Red Riding-Hood. My sympathies would be with the wolf.

She pressed the buzzer, waited a few seconds, then rapped on the glass.

Joyce opened it. Red Riding-Hood demanded Mr Barnes-Ingram. Joyce blinked behind her glasses and apologized. She didn't think Mr Barnes-Ingram could ... Red Riding-Hood dealt her a few choice verbal blows and Joyce retreated to see if Mr Barnes-Ingram might possibly ...

She sat down opposite me, lit a cigarette and left it to burn in the ashtray. She tapped her immaculate nails on the arm of the chair, picked up a magazine, looked at three pages, tossed it aside.

I was staring at her, mesmerized. She was beautiful, in a hard glossy way. Finally she looked towards me. She looked through me. Right through me without a flicker. I'd become one with the pot-plants, a sort of small, bushy red-leaved shrub. My black shoes were the roots. They were suitably grimy. Not *quite* the thing for Mr Barnes-Ingram's reception room.

Chloe drew back the glass. Mr Barnes-Ingram would be able to ...

When the coast was clear she raised her eyebrows at me and made a kind of la-di-da movement.

"Who's she?"

Chloe glanced over her shoulder, then motioned me over with a wiggle of her index finger.

"Your father's handling her divorce. Isn't she incredible? No appointment. Just sails in and wants the moon, with jam on it. Sorry, love. You're going to have a bit of a wait."

"Is she somebody famous?" I asked naïvely.

"Mrs Delaney? No, love, just filthy rich, although she'd probably like . . ."

"Miss Mackenzie?"

It was Miss Miller, emerging from her cubby-hole like a dragon from its lair.

"These are what you needed for the Jovanovich file."

She waved a sheaf of papers at Chloe, giving me a kindly smile. Reflected glory from Brian shone round my head like a halo.

In the wash-room, as I cleaned my paint-stained fingers, I remembered where I'd heard the name. The dark-haired man at Pamela's party had mentioned her. I shook off the bad memory of that night. It was over and done with.

Back in reception, I began day-dreaming about France. Mum had been there as a student. Now she was going to teach international students for ten days. She'd got me a place and I couldn't wait. My school summer project was on Renoir. I meant to get lots of postcard reproductions and take photos of Montmartre and other places where he'd worked.

Just Mum and me. It would be so good. I felt as if I was wearing a straitjacket when Brian was around. Our "family" holiday in Cornwall was something I didn't even want to think about. I wondered, not for the first time, if Mum might let me stay behind when the Campbells came down to use our house. The problem was that our holidays didn't overlap. I'd have to be on my own for a day or two till they arrived.

The woman in the red suit didn't come back. Some time later I heard heels clicking down the outer corridor and the soft thud of the street door closing. Then Brian came through from his office and we went to the car park, a gloomy place below street level.

Old Johnnie, the attendant, raised a hand in salute as we drove out. The traffic was heavy, and we had to wait. Brian switched on the radio and adjusted the volume control with one hand, while watching the stream of traffic for a gap.

"Brian, how old is Mr Davis?"

"Johnnie? Well into his seventies, I imagine. Get my sunglasses out, would you?"

I got them from the glove compartment and passed them over.

"Why doesn't he retire?"

"It would kill him," Brian said calmly. "He reads his newspaper, drinks tea. He's happier in his little cupboard here than he would be at home."

Brian swung the big Mercedes out quickly into the main road, and opened the sun roof. "Every year," he spoke louder against the traffic, "that fool George tries to persuade me to replace him with a younger man, and I refuse. His heart's as fragile as a cracked plate, but he's happy because he feels he's useful."

We turned on to Barber Street, where the lights were against us.

"You look mildly scandalized."

"Sorry?"

"From the expression on your face, I take it you disapprove. Or does my benevolence surprise you?"

I stared obstinately at the windscreen, pretending I didn't understand. It *had* surprised me. I hated being so obvious.

The lights changed to green. At the corner of Bemersyde Street and Printer's Row, he took the left-hand filter instead of the usual one.

"We're going the wrong way," I said.

"Not tonight, we're not."

"Where are we going?"

"Wait and see."

Just before the end of Park Gate, he slowed down, pulling the car in to the kerb.

"Right, I think this is it."

I got out. He locked the car and joined me on the pavement. We were next to "Atassi's", a shop I'd never been in. Nothing in the window had a price tag.

"Your mother said that you need clothes for this holiday."

"I don't. Anyway, this isn't my kind of . . ."

"She warned me it might be a struggle." He took me by the elbow and moved me towards the door.

"Be a good girl. For Paris you need something new," he urged, chivvying me through the door like a dog with a wayward sheep.

The sales assistant, slim and elegant, glanced at us then tactfully looked away. She began tidying an already tidy rack of coloured tights. In my school uniform I felt about as elegant as a baked bean.

"You might see something you like," Brian said encouragingly. "Chloe assured me this was the place. Come on, give it a try."

He coughed meaningfully. The assistant came over at once. She could have been Malayan. Her skin was dark honey and she had gorgeous slanting eyes. Her dress was a kind of dull green, like terre-verte paint. Not that it mattered. She'd have looked terrific in a potato sack.

Brian explained. Something for a holiday in Paris. She smiled at him, said, "Oh, how exciting!" and led me to the racks of dresses.

I clutched at the first white thing in my size, white being my "safe" colour. Stomping wasn't possible on the thick carpeting but inside I was stomping, all the way to the changing cubicle. I hated shops without price tags, and I hated being patronized.

The dress fitted. The price on the tag was JW/V. Secret code for the idle rich. I made a face at the girl in the mirror. Why are you letting him do this? I asked myself. This isn't you . . .

I stepped out of it gingerly and reached for my old black skirt, which looked hurt and crumpled.

"Hi there."

"Sorry?"

"May I?" The assistant drew back the curtain a little. "Your father thought this might suit you."

I said the white one was fine, but I took the other dress and closed the curtain.

"Ready yet?" she asked after a few moments.

"Oh, that's really good on you," she drew back the curtain and called Brian over.

I felt like a prize sheep in an auction ring, waiting for his comments. But, at the same time, I knew the dress made me look good. It wasn't what I'd have picked, and it looked like nothing on the hanger, but it was good on me. In fact it was perfect.

"Like it?"

"Yes," I said, hating myself for saying it. I wished I knew what he was thinking.

"Fine. We'll take it." He smiled at the assistant.

I struggled back into my uniform, and she took the dress away.

When I came out, she was handing over the receipt. I caught sight of an unbelievable price total. I felt hot and cold. He'd bought both of them.

As we drove home, my mind was whirling. I liked the dresses, but how could I ever wear them? It was ridiculous to pay so much for clothes. And I didn't want to take things from him. Why was he doing it anyway?

On the radio, the news programme ended, and Brian changed stations. More classical music. Never anything I wanted to hear. Suddenly my mind flew back to that evening in the spring when he'd been annoyed with me for wearing trousers. Now he'd bought me dresses. To please himself. Perfect step-daughters should wear dresses.

My step-father. The Man Who Married My Mother. It sounded like a cheap paperback book. I was losing touch, losing myself. Who was I? The Girl Who Was Too Young To Leave Home.

After the dual carriageway we began to wind along tree-shadowed lanes. The sun flickered through, hidden for a moment then dazzling our eyes as we changed direction. Mile after mile we rolled on, not speaking. Nothing in common. Nothing that really mattered.

Mum was just hanging up the telephone when we came in.

"Sorry we're late, darling," Brian began. "I think you'll approve when you see what we've . . ."

She ignored him.

"Jo," she said, clutching distractedly at her hair. What had happened? She looked really upset.

"Hey, we're OK, honestly. Brian took me shopping. He said you . . ."

"That was the Course Organizer. There's a problem."

"What's wrong?" I said quickly.

"I phoned to see why your documents hadn't come. I can't believe it. They didn't register you, because you're under sixteen."

# 3
# Chocolate brownies

The next couple of days were awful. Mum argued and pleaded with the London organizers and got nowhere. She even phoned Paris twice. They were full of regret, but there was nothing to be done. Sixteen was the age limit and, in any case, all the places were taken. She kept apologizing to me, which made it worse.

"I'm sorry. It's all my fault, I'm hopeless with forms," she said dismally, over and over again. It was true, but it didn't help. Then, when we'd accepted the inevitable, she had something new to say as we sat finishing our evening meal.

"I can't possibly go without Joanne," she announced. "It's out of the question. They'll have to get someone else. I'll tell them in the morning."

"You can't let them down, Anne," Brian objected.

"They've let *me* down," she countered. "Anyway, it's *my* decision, isn't it?"

He shrugged his shoulders and said no more.

Later on, he went upstairs to do some work, leaving Mum and me in the sitting room by ourselves. I was pretending to watch a "cops and robbers" film, and she was pretending to do a crossword. She never ever does crosswords. I felt I was going to burst if we didn't talk soon. I had to say something.

"You really want to go, don't you?"

"What, dear?"

"Paris. You still want to go."

Her smile wouldn't have fooled a blind man.

"I'll survive."

"Oh, Mum."

She leaned forward to pick a sweet paper off the carpet.

"Why am I the only person who ever picks up rubbish in . . ."

"Mum."

She sighed. "All right, I suppose I do." Her fingers smoothed the square of silver paper, then began to pinch the edges. "Maybe it's something to do with my next birthday." She sighed again. "Thirty-nine seems so old. Only one year to go . . ."

Why do they all panic at the idea of being forty? I wondered.

"But you've not gone flabby or anything," I said, trying to cheer her up.

"Not outside," she gave her stomach a couple of tentative slaps. "But inside? Inside, my lovie, I feel distinctly flabby. And my work's getting flabby. I know exactly what the thing's going to look like long before I'm finished. Of course, it's years since I was in France. It'll be all different I suppose . . ."

"I think you should go," I heard myself say. I was digging a pit for myself.

"It wouldn't be fair, dear. I couldn't."

"It's silly for you not to go."

"I'll do it another year. Next year. We'll go together."

But she was weakening. And because it had unsettled me to my bones to hear her speaking like that about

27

her painting, I hid my misery and jumped like a proud hero into the blazing pit. And that was that.

The Saturday after school ended, Mum went off to get a load of frozen food, so that Brian and I wouldn't starve to death. I wasn't dressed and she wouldn't wait.

"Much faster without you," she shouted upstairs. "Serves you right for wasting half the morning in bed."

Looking out of the window I could see Brian wrestling with the hedge. It was as old as the original farmhouse building. The estate agent had called it irreplaceable.

The house itself had been modernized inside, and the old dairy buildings, made into a workshop by the previous owner, were perfect for all Mum's painting gear.

The nearest house was a mile away across fields, two miles by the winding road. The village lay roughly a mile in the opposite direction. It was hard to imagine anything less like the terraced house and the city street I'd grown up in.

As Mum drove by in her battered but beloved white Fiat she stopped, wound down the window and shouted something. I heaved the bedroom window up.

"What?"

"I said, make Brian coffee. But don't do potatoes. I'll bring lunch back with me."

"OK," I yelled back, and she trundled cautiously away along the rather potholed road.

A little later I did my willing slave bit. It was warm outside. Brian was in his "I'm still young and fit" clothes – khaki shorts and a white sports shirt.

He looked hot. I held out the coffee and a plate of brownies.

"There's apple juice in the fridge . . ."

"Coffee's fine." He dropped the hedge cutter and stepped back out of the clippings.

"What d'you call these things?"

"Chocolate brownies."

"Are these what you were making last night?"

I nodded, watching him taste one.

"They're rather good. Clever you."

"They're easy."

"Mmm," he took another bite. "Easy for you creative types. People who get it right always insist it's easy. No, leave the plate."

He gave me a big smile. I smiled back. I put the plate down on top of the sundial, and turned towards the house, feeling rather pleased with myself.

Mum had left the breakfast dishes. I began to stack them. Then abruptly I saw how stupid I was. I suddenly understood why Miss Miller idolized him. Why Chloe did hours of overtime without complaining. He was so clever. He knew just where a person's ego was most vulnerable, where their weak spot was. It cost him nothing to toss compliments like crumbs in the right direction. Any moron could make chocolate brownies.

"Know something?" I told the three smiling characters on the Rice Krispie packet. "These are going to be the worst ten days of my entire life. Totally and utterly the very worst."

I abandoned the dishes. I gathered up my drawing things, stuffed a couple of apples and some cake on top of them in my bag and went out to tell Brian I was off.

"To the river? Fair enough," he gave the cutter a

short burst of power. "Just don't do any Ophelia imitations."

"Any what?"

"Don't fall in," he laughed at my ignorance.

"Our" river belonged to the neighbouring farm, as did the fields all round the house. It was easy to get to as long as Mr Wilson's black-and-white bullocks were elsewhere.

There was a small copse of beeches and young oaks, and fragile willows along the banks leaning towards the shallow water. It flowed slowly. Thick patches of white flowers grew out of it, and the weed below was like matted green hair, rippling up and down.

Every time I came to the river the shapes were different, or the light was different. I sketched for a long time, pastels on grey paper for a change, until my right leg went to sleep. I stamped around, then went nearer the water. It was hypnotic, a moving sheet of dimpled green-and-brown glass.

I crumbled a little bit of sponge into it. Either there were no fish, or chocolate brownie wasn't to their taste. There was a scent of something like onions in the air. The traffic on the distant main road made a muffled buzz. A cloud of tiny insects danced madly above the water.

I watched them, and the water sliding past, and my thoughts slid about in much the same way, until finally they settled on something I'd read that morning in my book of Bible verses. I didn't always read it, and I didn't always understand it either, but sometimes the words stuck. This morning there had been a verse that said: "If you fall, it isn't fatal, because the Lord holds you with his hand."

Out here, with no one else near me, shaded by the

willows and with the water rippling rhythmically at my feet, prayer was easier somehow. It seemed natural, like talking to a friend.

"Lord," I began, "are you really holding me? If you're holding me, why is everything so awful?"

The water rippled loudly on.

"Because it is awful, you know that, Lord? And," I swallowed, "I don't know how I'm going to get through this summer. I don't think I can do it."

I turned wearily back from the water. Turned, and saw somebody at my bag. Anger shot through me like a lightning bolt.

"Hey! Stop that!"

He straightened up. A fair-haired man, in scruffy clothes.

I didn't stop to think. Back over the flood dyke I clambered, hot with righteous indignation.

I thought he would run. He didn't. About three metres away I stopped. He wasn't a man. Just a boy. Not much older than me. Stockily built, broad in the shoulders.

He had one of my chocolate cakes in his mouth and was tossing an apple up and down. He watched me all the time.

"You leave my things alone. Get out of here. This is private property."

Not mine either, but he wasn't to know.

"Fancy that."

"I'll yell for my Dad."

"Hidin' under a bush is 'e?"

I didn't know what to do. Would Brian hear me?

"Come on, darlin'. Give us a break. Haven't had nothing since breakfast yesterday, have I?"

He took a bite out of the apple and chewed insolently. He was dirty all over; the T-shirt could have been white once, but it was frayed and streaked with dirt, as were the tight jeans. From the grime on his face and his hair, he looked as if he'd spent the night in a ditch. Where did he come from, with that accent?

"You live round here?"

"It's none of your business."

"Pretty fancy drawing," he stirred the sketch pad with his foot.

"Leave that alone, you . . .'

"All right, all right. No harm done. I'm going." He moved back as I darted forward to rescue my property.

"You got any money?"

Get away, I told myself, get away and get home. I started walking towards the trees.

Suddenly he bounded in front of me, barring my way. My anger flipped into fear.

"Look darlin', I need cash," his voice was wheedling, soft as butter. "You got some, you can 'ave this."

He held out his arm. The watch looked expensive; it could have been gold. Where had he got it? I stared. His wrist was strong-looking, like the rest of him. Fear closed my throat.

"Look, don't be shy. I don't need a lot, darlin'. I can't hang around here, get it? This mate of mine, see, he thinks I shopped him, which I didn't. But he's not a reasonable kind of fella, so he . . . Oh, you! Dumb brute!"

From the bushes a large animal suddenly came lumbering between us. A massive brown horse, with a huge rump and a black swishing tail: I backed into a beech tree. Quickly, the boy caught at the bridle. The horse tried to toss him off, but he held it firmly, talking all the time in a voice totally unlike his former one. In a moment it stopped fidgeting.

"Tequila, you pig, behave yourself," he said. He

caught sight of me, and grinned.

"She won't touch you. Not a bad old sort, are you sweetheart?" he said, stroking the beast's nose.

"Is there another apple, by any chance?"

He was mad. Or I was mad. Clutching my satchel, I ran like a demented banshee through the rest of the trees, stumbled over the fence, and hurtled across the tussocky field towards the house.

The Fiat was back. I collided with Mum in the kitchen doorway. Milk shot up, cascading from the open carton she'd been holding, drenching us both. From my satchel, crayons, brushes, tubes and cake crumbs flew like pieces from an exploding bomb.

Mum yelled at me and I burst into tears.

# 4
# Being a snail

Brian had heard the yell. He came hurriedly through from the downstairs bathroom, clad only in shorts, rubbing his hair with a towel.

"What's happened?"

I was silly with tears, mopping at the work-surface with soggy kitchen towels, doing no good. Mum was on her knees picking up paint tubes.

"I don't know, dear. Joanne's had a fright. She says she met a young tramp in the woods."

Brian dropped the towel on to the kitchen table and strode out.

"Listen, lovey, it's all right. Brian will see him off." She put a reassuring arm round my heaving shoulders.

". . . wasn't . . . tramp," I stuttered.

"Well, whoever. Come and sit down. We'll do that in a minute." She took the disintegrating paper from me, and made me sit.

"Don't you move. I'm going to change, I'm soaked," she said, smiling to show she wasn't angry.

Moments later she came back in a different blouse and skirt, with a dry sweatshirt for me too, and while she mopped the floor, she gradually got the story out of me.

"Your guess is as good as mine," she said finally.

"But you are all right, aren't you? He didn't hurt you?"

"He was filthy, Mum." I grimaced at the memory.

She gave the cloth a final rinse. The air was full of the harsh lemon smell of the cleaning liquid. She hadn't put her hair up after breakfast, and now the long plait down her back was dark and sticky-looking where the milk had soaked it.

"I'll phone Mr Wilson if Brian doesn't find anyone. He could be a casual worker."

"But what about the horse?"

"Perhaps it's from the farm."

"Mr Wilson hasn't got horses."

She frowned. Then smiled brightly.

"Anyway. Lunch. Ham salad. You do the cucumber."

She passed me a knife. We grated cheese, put coleslaw into a dish, tossed the salad, laid out the cold ham. All the time I was waiting for the door to open.

When it did, we both jumped like nervous rabbits. She'd been as tense as me.

"Well?"

"No problem."

"Did you find anyone?"

"Yup."

"So what happened?"

"Is there a shirt of mine in here?" Brian rifled through the basket of clothes on top of the fridge.

"Those aren't ironed yet, and would you please stop fooling about. What happened, Brian?" Mum said sharply.

His head emerged through the top of a red sports shirt.

"Nothing happened," he said mildly. "I caught up with Joanne's 'tramp' at the bridge where he was passing the time of day with the postman. Mr Robinson introduced us. We had a pleasant discussion about the state of the river after . . ."

"But how did Mr Robinson . . ." Mum began.

". . . last week's heavy rain," he went on, ignoring her. "Then I raised the subject of our whey-faced maiden here . . ."

"And?"

"And he apologized very nicely. Said he was sorry the horse had unsettled you, Joanne. I can see why it did," he reached for a slice of cucumber. "Fifteen hands if it's an inch. Is there soup or just salad?"

I found my voice.

"But who . . . I mean, it was him, not the horse. It was him. He was filthy. And crude."

"I admit he wasn't in pristine condition, but I hardly think 'crude' an appropriate word to describe the son of the village's most distinguished resident."

Mum and I looked blankly at him.

"Our world-famous conductor, Carl Niemenen. The son's called Peter. Now, are we having lunch today or are we not?"

"Oh, Joanne," Mum bit her lip and began to giggle. But it wasn't funny.

"I'm not hungry," I said abruptly. They exchanged smiles. I couldn't bear it. Mum began to speak but I ran off, pounding up the stairs to the safety of my bedroom.

I felt like breaking something. I picked up a pencil. Finally it snapped, but I still felt mad. Mad and stupid. I flung myself on to the bed, wanting to cry, but I couldn't even get tears to come. When I closed my eyes, all I saw was that boy barring my way, making a fool of me. I smelled the horse and felt its tail threshing in my face.

I turned over. Above me, on the wall beside the

bed, hung a print I'd had for years, Renoir's "Path going up into the high grass". A sloping sun-bleached hill, softly coloured in shades of fawn and blue. Small dark-leaved trees. A bright path in the middle. There was a beautiful woman, turning to face me, half-way up the path. She held an open red parasol behind her white hat. Nearby, a little girl in a dark dress and a yellow straw hat had paused to catch a butterfly. I loved that print. I suppose I'd always thought it was Mum and me.

The door opened.

"Anybody home?"

I sat up, brushing the hair from my face.

"Come and have lunch, angel."

"I'm not hungry," I told her.

She came right in and closed the door. I lay back down and stared at the ceiling.

"What's the matter?"

"Nothing."

"If something happened at the river . . ."

"Nothing happened."

She was silent for a few moments.

"I don't understand what's got into you. I wish you would talk to me, Joanne," she said finally.

I raised myself on one elbow.

"I do talk to you. This is talking, isn't it?"

"Is it? Sometimes I think we only talk *at* one another these days. And the harder I try . . ." she rubbed at her eyebrow. Then she sighed.

"You're retreating from us. Like a snail. Whenever anyone touches your antennae you retreat in a panic."

"Great, now I'm a snail. You say the nicest things."

"You're not listening to me . . ."

"Well, *you* never listen to *me* any more!"

It came out too fast. I couldn't stop it.

37

Her eyes narrowed. "So it's all *my* fault? I suppose *I'm* the one who orders you to slope off here every night as soon as dinner's finished? Do I? Well?"

I studied the ceiling.

"And if you won't let Betty do this room, you might at least clean it yourself once in a while. Cleanliness *is* supposed to be next to godliness, or so they say."

With that she went. She didn't exactly slam the door, but it felt as if she had.

A snail, she'd called me. I felt more like something caught by a spider, trussed in a sticky web. OK, so we didn't talk any more. Too true. But how could we? What could I honestly say that didn't begin with, "Why did you have to marry him?" And that last bit about the state of the room. That didn't bother her. She was really getting at my faith. Why did that annoy her? She hadn't liked it when I tried to explain, so now I didn't even try to talk about Jesus. Why was she still irritated? I couldn't win. It was *my* room. She didn't even have to come into it. And it was *my* faith. I couldn't change that to please her.

# 5

# One hundred per cent crazy

On the Sunday I went to the evening service in the village, glad to get out of the house. Mum was packing and Brian was in a bad mood because he'd mislaid some papers.

Mr Caldicott, the vicar, was a thin washed-out looking man, with faded grey hair and rimless specs. He never seemed very sure who I was. His smile at the door was kind but vague. Perhaps it confused him to see someone under fifty in his church.

Even when I didn't understand his talks, I always felt better for going. The church was old and musty, but it was peaceful, and the stained glass was beautiful. One showed a dark-haired knight in pale grey armour, kneeling at the feet of Jesus. The sunlight sometimes shone through the ruby colour of Jesus's robes, spilling on to the stone floor.

Apart from polite nods, none of the old people spoke to me as we went out. They had lived here for decades after all. What was nine months? Rain had been pattering on the roof all through the service, but the clouds had moved on. Outside, the dark yews in the graveyard were furred with wetness. Straggling rose bushes sagged into the path, wetting my sandalled feet.

Directly across from the church was the village garage with its single petrol pump. Water streamed like liquid silver from a break in the guttering. A large black car had stopped for petrol, its sills dripping with tiny rain pearls.

I held the gate for Miss Peters, the Post Office lady, and her aged mother. How alike they were. More like sisters. Stout, beaky-nosed, smiling and nodding, in light fawn raincoats and paisley-patterned scarves.

We exchanged good evenings. Miss Peters' ear-rings glinted modestly in the evening sunlight. The old lady rummaged in her handbag for a handkerchief. Life went on as it always would. They smiled politely, and turned up the hill towards the Post Office.

I turned in the other direction. Rivulets of rainwater patterned the tarmac. What would it be like to live all your life with just one person, through childhood, youth, and middle age, dressing the same way, and doing everything together? I shivered.

Had Miss Peters never felt like rebelling? Even to the extent of a different headscarf? She could have gone crazy and bought a hat. I wondered if she was happy. Had life turned out the way she wanted it to?

"Hey!"

A yell from behind interrupted my thoughts.

"Hey! Want a lift?"

Puzzled, I stared at the shouting figure. I didn't recognize him. He bent to speak to the driver of the black car then, as he loped towards me, recognition came, too late. It was the boy from yesterday! I began to walk quickly downhill.

"Hey, wait," he bounded alongside me, making me stop. "It's going to pour again in a minute," he gestured at the sky. "We'll give you a lift."

"I like walking and rain doesn't bother me."

He shrugged his shoulders.

"Fine by me."

He fell into step beside me. I stopped.

"What do you think you're doing?"

"I like walking too."

"What about your father?"

"What about him?" He looked puzzled.

"In the car. Won't he miss you dreadfully?"

My attempt at sarcasm fell flat.

"Do me a favour. Larry's the chauffeur."

I moved away. He came too.

"Was it fun?"

"Look, I don't want company, so why don't you . . ."

"I can think of maybe ten fun ways to brighten a boring Sunday, but going to church? You can't be that desperate. Even in this moribund village, there has to be more on offer. From a statistical point of view, you're probably among . . ."

The car drew alongside.

Down slid the window. Larry the chauffeur looked at us through dark glasses. Black hair, combed straight back, and a black beard, greying a little. For no good reason at all, the word "Mafia" rose instantly in my mind like a genie from an unstopped bottle. Perhaps because he looked so out of place. Or it could have been the blackness of his tie against the white shirt that unsettled me. Perfect for garotting pedestrians who blocked his way on country lanes.

"I'm walking."

"Where to?" asked the man.

"That's my business."

"Your father pays me to make it my business, Master Peter."

I glanced at Peter. The joking smiles had vanished. I couldn't read the welter of emotions in his eyes as

41

he stared back at the man. Anger? Or was there fear too?

The seconds ticked on. A bird nearby sounded unnaturally loud.

"We're only going as far as the bridge," I said, astonishing myself.

Larry angled his glasses towards me. One black eyebrow rose briefly. His eyes could have been any colour behind the glass.

I felt Peter's hand close on mine.

"Then I'll wait at the crossroads."

"You do that," Peter said tightly.

The window slid up and the car drew away from us. We watched it for a few seconds. Then the spell broke. Quickly I drew my hand out of Peter's.

He lifted his thoughtfully.

"I'll never wash this hand again."

"So you do wash? Now and again? Or was the other day your normal appearance?"

"Yesterday was Tequila's fault. She threw me into a ploughed field. But if you want to know the truth," he waggled his eyebrows mysteriously, "actually I'm a wizened old gnome with a toothless grin. When rain-water falls upon my visage, as it did a moment ago, I step forth as the suave, incredibly handsome fellow you see before you. Don't laugh," he held up a hand in protest, "You mustn't laugh. If a maiden laughs at me I turn back into a gnome. Horrible, horrible . . .'

He clutched at his sweater, and made his voice go hoarse, as if the transformation was beginning. I had to giggle.

I was two people at once. The sensible part of me was saying, you don't know this boy and you don't want to after his crazy behaviour a day ago. The other

42

part was excited because he was good looking, now the coating of mud had gone. And he was different. And his father was famous.

"What's your name, anyway?"

"Joanne Fletcher."

"Try again. That wasn't the name your father told me yesterday."

"Step-father."

"Ho hum," he picked up a stone and shot it at the telephone wires, "so that's how the land lies." He reached for another stone, and missed again.

"Does he beat you?"

It was such a stupid question, I didn't know how to reply.

"Well, does he?"

"Of course not."

"Lucky you. When did you move here?"

"November."

"Like it?"

"Yes, mostly."

"I hate it mostly, but I'm away at Borstal mostly so I only have to endure holidays mostly. Boarding school," he added, in response to my startled expression.

We were half-way down the hill. Beyond the bridge the big car waited on the grass verge, crouching like a shiny black insect.

"I suppose you've heard of my father," he said abruptly.

"Yes."

I couldn't think what else to say without showing how little I knew about music.

"I hate his guts."

He meant to shock me, and he did.

"Not that it bothers him," he went on airily, "since

43

he never lingers in my presence long enough to find out. So it doesn't matter really."

Fat bees buzzed in and out of the dog roses in the hedge beside us. From the field beyond came the rasping noise of cows tearing up grass for supper. I stared at him. His voice and his eyes were saying different things.

"His public adore him, which has to be what counts. Don't look at me like that. I suppose you're a loyal fan. Forget I said it."

I looked away.

"Forget it. We have met but twice and we may never meet again. Let us, fair Joanne Fletcher, be as ships that pass in the night, swept apart for ever by the currents of time and . . . You're crying."

"No, I'm not."

I tried to find a tissue. My pocket was full of shredded bits.

"Why on earth are you crying?"

How could I tell him? I hardly knew myself.

"Oh, here, use mine." He thrust a folded hankerchief at me. "Keep it," he added, when I offered it back. "Give it away to Oxfam or something."

"I'll wash it," I mumbled inanely.

We were at the bridge. I didn't say goodbye. I clattered over the rusty poles of the cattle grid. At the corner of the track, beside the oak with the fungus on it, I turned to look, but he'd gone.

There was a light on in the outhouse. I guessed that Mum had gone in to do some last-minute work. In the house, Brian was reading in front of the television, his document case on the coffee table and papers strewn around. I said, "I'm back." He grunted without looking up.

I filled a mug with apple juice and took it out to the back garden. The seat was damp, so I leaned against the house wall. Strong evening scents filled the garden, especially from the roses.

Peter Niemenen's handkerchief made a bulge in my pocket. Why had I cried? It was nothing to me if he hated his father, nothing. Why had he said it anyway? What kind of person told strangers that kind of thing? He was different all right. He was crazy. One hundred per cent crazy.

The roughcast was needling into my shoulder blades through my thin blouse, and my bare toes were cold in the wet grass. The sky before me was paler than a sparrow's egg. When I walked round, the setting sun was colouring the other side of the house a pale cadmium red.

I could imagine what Peter Niemenen might be thinking about me. "Frightens easily; cries easily; religious nut." An emotional cripple, with religion for a crutch. It wasn't how I saw myself, but was that how I really was?

He hated his father, or so he said. But how could he say it didn't matter? That was a lie, even if he didn't admit it to himself. It wasn't that simple. Maybe it felt like hatred to him but I wondered if it might not be what love turned into when the door slammed in its face too often.

I went back for the empty mug, then turned towards the house. More and more I found myself sidetracked like this — thinking about my feelings, turning them over, looking at different sides of them, and trying to fit them into a pattern that made sense. I couldn't just feel things about people these days without wondering whether how I felt about them was right or wrong. For someone like Peter Niemenen, it was probably a whole lot easier. I couldn't imagine him wasting a minute wondering whether it was right or wrong to feel like that about his father.

I meant to slip upstairs, but Mum heard me and called me into the sitting-room.

"That was a long service."

"I've been back a while. I was watching the sunset."

"I cut out an article from the paper for you. About the link between Renoir's rheumatism and the pigments he used. It's over there."

I crossed to the bookshelf. Brian was engrossed in the TV news and protested as I blocked his view. I slid into an armchair, and scanned the article.

Brian turned the volume up. The camera panned over the remains of a burnt-out car. There were jerky shots of stone throwers, and men running from others in helmets, with sirens sounding in the background.

"Where is this?" Mum asked.

"New York, I think. I missed the first part."

"As long as it's not Paris," she sat back in her chair. "I just missed the riots twenty years ago. We were annoyed at the time, because we'd left before it started. Can you imagine? I'd hate to get caught up in something like that now."

"I wouldn't worry, darling," Brian observed drily, "they're all running the country now."

"Who are?" I said, mystified.

"The students who were digging up cobble-stones in the Boulevard Saint Michel twenty-odd years ago. Most of them are now tossing memos at harassed civil servants."

"Did you ever wear beads, Brian?"

He looked at Mum in amazement.

"I most certainly did not."

"But everybody did."

"Possibly in your art college, Anne. At Oxford they didn't."

"Some did, Brian," she said indignantly. "I know some did. I had a friend, Jane . . . what *was* her name? Her cousin Nigel came to our flat once and he . . ."

When they started talking about The Past, I wanted to hide elsewhere. They could go on for ages. Twenty years even.

I watched the screen. Tanks were moving along streets somewhere. A map appeared, with a star beside Petroza-something. In Karelia, wherever that was.

Then came the sports news. That did distract Brian from his argument. Once it finished, he switched channels, into the middle of an old film.

"Excellent," he exclaimed, "I forgot this was on."

"What is it?"

*"She Wore A Yellow Ribbon."*

Mum made a face.

"It's a classic, darling." He patted the seat beside him invitingly. "John Wayne after all."

She looked at me as if to say, what can we do with him?

"I think I'll have a bath, if nobody minds," I said.

Nobody minded. I had a bath and went to bed. Nobody missed me.

# 6

# A shame to waste the sunshine

The morning after Mum left I woke in a panic. My dream had been so real. We'd been in the Fiat, driving towards our old house. The way was blocked with barricades of burning cars. Crowds were shouting, throwing stones and bottles.

Mum said she'd talk to the rioters. She was wearing beads, so they wouldn't hurt her. I tried to follow, knowing she was going to be hurt, but my hand got jammed in the door. When I woke, it was numb because I'd been lying on it.

Don't be stupid, I told myself. She's perfectly safe. The plane even landed on time. But the uneasy feeling wouldn't go away.

I reached for my little red book of Bible verses, feeling that I needed help, and hoping there would be something there that made sense. Right at the bottom of the page there was.

"Our hearts ache," it said, "but at the same time we have the joy of the Lord."

That helped a bit. I began to calm down. It dawned on me that it was all right to feel upset about saying goodbye to her and being left behind. Which in a way was pretty obvious. But I'd been panicking. That was wrong. After I'd read through the page of verses again, I still felt miserable, but things seemed to get into focus again somehow, and I prayed for Mum, that God would look after her, and I prayed for me, that I could get some of the joy as well as the aching.

Sunlight filtered through the slats of my blind, making interesting stripes on the ceiling. Another beautiful day, and I didn't want to get up. How would Brian react if I stayed in bed till Mum came home in ten days' time?

When a hoover began droning loudly below me, I realized that Betty, Mum's cleaning lady, had arrived. I stretched for the clock. Nearly ten. Brian would be in court by now. I went slowly downstairs, meeting Betty on the bottom landing.

"Oh, sorry, pet." She switched off the machine.

"I was waking anyway," I assured her, thinking, it just has to be a wig. Above her cheerful, wrinkled face the brown curls never varied.

The kitchen was awash with sunshine, the floor warm under my bare feet. The people before us had decorated the walls with pale lemon paint above white tiles, bordered with a tiny yellow, white and navy pattern. The units were plain white, and the table in the middle was plain unvarnished wood. Usually I loved the kitchen, but today it felt empty. The cornflakes tasted stale. I thought about French croissants and coffee, and pushed the bowl away.

Betty had worked for the previous owners, and Brian had asked her to "do" for us once a week too. I suppose it did make life easier, because none of us was tidy by nature, and Brian went crazy if things got mislaid. She'd agreed to come more often while Mum was away.

It was a mystery to me how anyone could enjoy

cleaning a house, but Betty loved it. She came through to the kitchen for her tea later on, but even then she did some ironing at the same time. Her freckled arm swished back and forth, subduing the creases.

"Your Mum's left me nice clear instructions about what she wants done for your Scottish visitors next week. Wednesday, isn't it?"

"I'm not sure what time. They're going to phone."

I thought about the Campbells coming and my heart sank a little further, because I wouldn't see them. We'd be in Cornwall. It wasn't fair.

"That's fine. You'll know by next Monday, I expect. I'll not do the beds till then. Anything else you want washed, pet?" she added. "It's a shame to waste the sunshine."

I found a shirt and three socks under the bed, took them down then went upstairs to stare out at the morning. My thoughts drifted back to the view I'd looked out on the previous summer in Scotland. I had paintings and sketches of it down in Mum's workroom, but I didn't need them. When I closed my eyes I could see morning sunlight shimmering on the grey sea loch, with the dark hills rising beyond.

I imagined I could hear Neil in the vegetable patch, yelling at his brother to come and help. I saw Roddy thinking it over, cleaning his glasses with a piece of kitchen paper, then having to duck as Neil threw a clump of weeds at him.

One night we'd had a bonfire down on the shore. We'd eaten baked potatoes and slightly burnt sausages, with ice-cold apple juice, avoiding the sparks and laughing ourselves silly. I couldn't remember now what we'd been laughing at. When I thought about Neil and Roddy Campbell, a terrible lump rose in my throat. They were the brothers I'd never had. Roddy was easy to talk to, and Neil was fun. He could get me mad faster than anybody else, but I'd even begun to learn how to cope with that, once we'd all got to know one another better. I'd felt so happy last summer, and now it was all gone.

Reluctantly, I dragged myself back to the present and began to dress. I was washing my face when the phone rang.

Covered in bubbles, I belted through to Mum's bedroom, in case it was long-distance from Paris.

"Good morning, madam. I'm calling on behalf of Easy Care Home Laundries."

"Pardon?"

"Easy Care Home Laundries. Our representatives are in your area and we would like to interest you in our special terms this month . . ."

"I don't think we . . ."

". . . for curtains, chair covers, table linen. Of course, we also specialize in small items like handkerchiefs."

The penny dropped as his voice came down half an octave to normal. Peter.

"How did you get this number?"

"Simple, Watson. Directory Enquiries. Not a lot of Barnes-Ingrams about this summer. Must be the cold winds from Iceland, altering the flight patterns."

"If you want your handkerchief, it's just newly gone in the wash." I sat down on the fleecy rug beside the bed.

"Forget it. What're you busy doing?"

"Washing my face."

"Your face? Well, let me check our price list. Let me see . . . No, I'm sorry, we don't do faces. I'm afraid we can't help you there. Must get on to the management about that one."

"Don't let me hold you back."

51

"Hey, don't hang up," he said hurriedly. "If you're not doing anything, come and have lunch."

"What?" I squawked.

"Lunch. In about an hour."

"Where?"

"Here, of course."

"I couldn't."

"Of course you could. Go and ask Mummy."

"That's a bit difficult. She's in Paris."

"How the old folk get around. Ask Tarzan then."

"Who?"

The conversation was getting beyond me.

"Your step-father."

"His name is Brian, actually."

"Is it? Must have been the shorts. Never mind. Look, come at half twelve."

"I can't."

"Yes you can. Our kitchens are spotless and fully automated, apart from Mrs Burchfield. First class results guaranteed every time. Chicken pilaff today. I just asked her."

The food didn't worry me. How could I put it without being rude?

". . . and anyway, I said to Karen you'd come."

"Don't tell me, let me guess. Karen is your pet cockroach."

"She's my sister. She'd like to meet you. Please come."

His voice had gone serious. I felt hot. Why had I tried to be funny? Then I was annoyed. Why couldn't he have said who she was to begin with? Why did he have to make a pantomime out of everything?

"It's the house with the green gates."

"I might not get away," I began, but he'd already put the phone down.

I fluffed the rug up where I'd twisted it into lumps, and went downstairs.

Betty was elbow-deep in blue rubber gloves and pine disinfectant, attacking the downstairs toilet.

Of course she knew Mrs Burchfield. She was the housekeeper at Low Woods. Treasurer of the Women's Institute this year. Why did I ask?

"They've just invited me for lunch."

She looked puzzled.

"Mary Burchfield invited you?"

I explained.

"But I don't think I should go . . ."

"Why not, pet? Do you good to have some company."

"He wants me to meet his sister."

"Does he? That's nice." She turned back to her scrubbing.

A thought struck me.

"Is the chauffeur Mrs Burchfield's husband?"

"What, pet?"

"A man with a black beard. I saw him the other day."

"Black beard? Can't say I've seen him. No, Mary's a widow. Her mother worked there when the old gentleman was alive. This one's a foreigner, German or something."

She dropped the cloths into a basin, checked that the top of the disinfectant was tight, and began tidying the things on the shelves.

Just after twelve I heard her calling to say she was finished for now, and would see me later. I waved as she cycled off down the road. Then I didn't know what to do. None of the things I'd thought of doing around the house seemed interesting. Outside the birds were going crazy and the sun was high. The sister might be worth meeting, since I never saw any of my school friends in the holidays now. There was no harm in going. Anyway, it was more fun than cooking my own lunch.

# 7

# Master Peter

The gates were set in a high stone wall but they weren't locked so I wheeled my clanking bike through. My heart was thumping, and when something whisked across the drive in front of me I gasped in fright. But it was only a grey squirrel. Its tail followed it into a tall chestnut tree.

Round the bend, the bushes thinned. A paddock on the right sloped down to more trees, and to the same river that later ran near our house. A donkey and two horses were leisurely chewing their way across the grass.

I'd expected the house to be bigger. It didn't look very grand: weatherbeaten red brick with red pantile roofs, trees behind to shelter it from the north. I clanked towards it, alongside a low lavender hedge seething with agitated bees.

As I got nearer I saw that there were other parts built on. It *was* big, big and sprawling. There was a verandah, with unfinished wooden timbers supporting the big triangular roof. Below its red brick wall a wheelbarrow sat with a rake jutting out, but there was no sign of a gardener. On the other side of the lavender, the lawn was like velvet, as if no one heavier than the bees ever trod on it.

Somewhere, very faintly, a radio was playing. I hesitated. Which was the front door?

Suddenly one of the lower windows swung open.

"Hello!"

I called hello back, and watched Peter swing himself out over the window ledge, jump down into the shrubs and bound out to meet me on the path.

"I'll take it," he said, taking the handlebars.

"I can manage."

"No charge, all part of the service."

Then it seemed neither of us could think of anything to say. We walked round to the side of the house, past the verandah, and he stood the bike against a wall. His shirt was pale grey, short-sleeved, his denims white with a grey belt. His hair looked different. He'd had it cut, and he'd obviously just washed it because the back was still damp.

I thought of the two new dresses hanging in my room. My navy T-shirt wasn't quite in the same league. His sister would probably look like something out of *Vogue*. A little voice told me I shouldn't have come.

"I expect you'd like to see the house."

"Is there time?"

"I'll tell Mrs B."

"What about your sister?" I said, meaning, shouldn't I introduce myself?

"No problem. Mrs B brings her through."

It seemed an odd thing to say.

"How old is she?"

"Goodness knows. The other side of fifty, but I suppose she wouldn't admit . . ."

"Your sister?" My voice squeaked incredulously.

"Oh, Karen? She's eight. Right, give me a minute."

My face fell. He saw it and assumed I was upset at the idea of being left behind.

"Well, come if you like. Why not? View the toiling millions."

He talked on about Mrs B and her cooking. I didn't hear him. I was too busy kicking myself. An eight-year-old. Here was the sister I'd thought I might get friendly with!

I followed him into a cool passageway, through two doors and into a large white-tiled kitchen. Millions was an exaggeration. There was only one person, Mrs Burchfield herself. A tall grey-haired woman, she was talking to someone on the telephone. Peter didn't wait till she'd finished. He announced that he was going to show me the house, so could lunch wait for . . . he checked his watch . . . another twenty minutes.

She put her hand over the telephone, saying "Pleased to meet you, Miss," and, "Just as you like, Master Peter". Her look was chilly. I couldn't have spoken to Betty like that to save my life.

I followed him back through the corridor into the main house. Everything was spotless. The walls were pale cream, with exposed oak beams. Parquet floors smelled faintly of polish. Little rectangles of priceless Persian carpet lay here and there. Faded pen-and-ink drawings hung on the walls in dark or gilt frames. Ferny plants stood in wicker baskets on wide window ledges.

He only showed me the downstairs rooms. He would fling open a door, saying, "This is the breakfast room," or "This is the dining-room," and I'd have all of twenty seconds to admire it before we were off again.

We came to a book-lined room with framed photographs on one wall. Carl Niemenen with lots of other famous people. Shaking hands with Yehudi Menuhin.

Arms round an elderly man I didn't recognize. I peered closer. "Arthur Rubinstein".

"This is when you're supposed to say how much I look like my father."

I turned.

"Am I?"

"Everyone else does. Good-looking guy, isn't he?"

He wasn't fishing for compliments. His tone was hard.

"You don't look like your mother at all," he continued.

"How would you know?"

"Saw her yesterday. Having lunch with Tarzan in town. In that Italian place in Hanover Street."

"You couldn't have. I told you, she's in Paris. And Brian was in court all day."

"If you say so."

Had he seen Brian? I doubted it. Peter had only met Brian once, so it was probably someone who looked like him from a distance. It wasn't worth arguing about.

The room was dominated by a grand piano. The wood was a warm honey instead of dark. It was open and I almost touched a note, but something stopped me.

"Can you play?" I turned to Peter.

"Of course."

He sat down, flexed his fingers, then leaned forward.

Tum tum tum, tum tum tum . . . He sat back from the keys.

"What was that?" I said, bewildered.

" 'Jingle Bells'. I thought it was quite good."

"I knew it was 'Jingle Bells'. I meant play something. Proper music."

"Sorry, honey chile." His voice took on the accent of the Deep South. " 'Jingle Bells' is as propah as we can do." He struck a single note. It hung sourly in the silence.

"But . . . I mean, your father . . ."

"Yes, appalling isn't it." He dropped the phoney voice. "The finest interpreter of Sibelius this century, and his son is tone deaf. Appalling."

Peter swung off the stool abruptly.

"Come on, there's not much more."

We entered a sitting-room. Warm light streamed through the windows. There was a strong smell of pot-pourri. Roses.

"Here, have a nut."

He picked up some walnuts from a bowl on a low table, cracked them and tossed two halves at me before I could say no. Then he up-ended himself without warning on a sofa, his legs up over the back of it. Three rose-pink scatter cushions slipped down to the carpet.

"You'll choke," I protested.

"Probably," he said cheerfully. "What do you think of the house?"

He stretched backwards for more nuts and the crackers, taking twice as long to get them as he would have if he'd got up.

What did I think of the house? There was no newspaper crumpled beside the armchair, no mug with a left-over trickle of cold coffee. No stray sock behind the cushion. No mess. Apart from the shells he was now tossing inaccurately towards the bowl.

"It's beautiful."

"Beautiful? Oh, isn't it just," Peter agreed. "Everything in simply perfect taste, from floor to ceiling. Simply, simply perfect."

His tone jarred. I could feel the last grains of liking for him trickling away fast. He wanted shaking, or a vase of cold water in his face or something.

The wallpaper and the matching curtains were cream with a faint pink pattern. I hadn't seen pink anywhere else.

"Is this your mother's room?"

"No," he said sharply.

He came upright again, still sitting. He didn't look at me, but stared instead at the crushed shells on the pale fawn carpet.

He sat like that for ages. I didn't know what to do. What had I said? It was like walking in a minefield. How much longer could I stand this?

"Are we going to eat?"

My words seemed to bring him back from very far away.

"Look," I added, "if you want me to go, I'll go."

He looked surprised.

"No," he said swiftly. "We'll eat now."

He opened the French windows and led the way along a stone-flagged path with a high hedge on the right. We had to unlatch a low gate. He paused with his hand on it.

"I should have said . . ." he began. He scratched at a flake of varnish with his thumb-nail.

"I assumed you would know. My mother died when Karen was born."

"Oh. I'm sorry. I wouldn't have . . . I'm sorry."

"Yes. Well. If no one told you . . ."

"It must have sounded . . . I didn't mean to . . ."

"Forget it."

He pushed the gate open, and held it for me.

"I'm so sorry."

"Why?"

"Because . . ." I faltered under the directness of his look.

"Because she died? So what's new? Everybody dies."

We were at the side gate of a conservatory, built on to the house wall. The door resisted him. He had to put his shoulder to it.

"Here's another . . ." he gave it a shove, "little job . . ." another shove and it gave, "for dear Larry. The rain last week must have swollen the wood. Warm in here, isn't it?"

The moment had gone. We were back on the surface. Anything I might have said about death or about God would have been a non-starter. But some time I'd tell him. Some time when the moment was right. I felt a bit shaky inside. His cynical pose was exactly that. A front. My chance mention of his mother had hurt, just for a few perilous seconds. Now the steel shutters were up again.

"I thought Larry was the chauffeur."

"Chauffeur, handyman, mechanic. You name it, he does it. He's wonderfully capable, our Larry. In his two short weeks here, he has quelled the gardener, flirted with the cleaning lady, and won Mrs Burchfield's heart."

"But not yours?"

"You bet your sweet freckled nose, not mine."

"He made me think of the Mafia," I ventured.

"You've got it,' he nodded encouragingly. "You have got it in one." He brushed his sleeve where the doorpost had soiled it.

"He's a creep. Every time I turn round, he's breathing down my neck. About the only thing I get to do on my own is go to the bathroom."

There was a table set for lunch at the end of the

conservatory. I saw we were on the other side from where I'd arrived. A door opened into another passage from here to the kitchen. Peter went off to tell Mrs Burchfield we were ready.

The door to the garden was open. Here the lawn sloped down to the dark trees whose tops I'd glimpsed on the way up the drive. I breathed the smell of warm earth and the strong scent of scarlet geraniums on the shelf beside me. Their leaves left a bitter smell on my fingers.

Peter came back, and Mrs Burchfield followed with a trolley full of salads and different meats. I saw chicken but no pilaff. Perhaps it had spoiled.

Without speaking, she set out bread rolls and small dishes of relishes. I felt faintly embarrassed when Peter talked on about the awful food he got at school, as if she wasn't there. As she finished, he said, "Bring Karen now, Mrs Burchfield."

"She might not come," she said levelly.

He looked at her. She shrugged her broad shoulders and turned away.

"Butter?"

"No, thank you. What did she mean?"

"Is that all the chicken you want? Have some more."

He didn't answer my question. He asked what my school was like and told me more about his. He said he'd sat exams at the end of term, but didn't expect to pass. I said I supposed everyone felt like that; he replied that, not having done a stroke of work, he was entitled to feel fairly certain.

He wanted to know what Brian did for a living, although he persisted in calling him Tarzan.

"I'm not sure he looks like a lawyer," he mused. "My father's lawyer's about eighty, with a stomach measurement to match. And he takes snuff."

"Is your father German?"

"German? No, he's a Finn. Well, to be accurate," he refilled his glass from the bottle of mineral water, "he's probably Russian. It's an interesting story. This house belonged to my maternal grandfather. But I also have a grandfather I've never met, in Karelia. That's part of Russia, just across the border from Finland. My grandmother ended up with Father in the Finnish part after the war. Grandfather stayed on the Russian side. She never saw him again."

"That's terrible."

He shrugged slightly.

"Maybe it wasn't much of a marriage. Or maybe he was a loyal party man. I know he's still alive, but that's about it. Father never speaks about him."

"Isn't that the place they're having all those demonstrations?"

"Are they?" He lifted the salad bowl. "Do you want more of this, or shall I finish it? Karen never eats lettuce."

"It was on the news the other night. I'm sure they said Karelia. They want to get independence from Moscow, I think."

"Could be. I don't watch the box much. Rots the brain."

"Speaking of boxes," Peter added after a moment's pause. He leant over backwards so that his chair nearly overbalanced. He picked up a small package from the ledge. "Saw this yesterday. I had to walk around while Karen had her turn under the scissors. For you," he said, pushing it nearer.

"What for?"

"Birthday," he said, through a mouthful of salad.

"My birthday was in March."

He snapped his fingers.

"Bother! I knew I'd missed it."

"Oh don't be stupid."

"Well, open it. Go on."

I opened it.

"I . . . I can't take this from you."

"Well, *I'm* not going to wear it. Try it on."

I slid the bangle on to my wrist. Circles of pale-blue stones set in what had to be silver. It looked expensive. I put it back on to the nest of cotton wool. My stomach was churning. I could feel my face going pink. I didn't know how to handle this.

"Don't you . . ." he began, then stopped. Mrs Burchfield was with us, framed by the doorway.

"She doesn't want to come," she said quietly.

"Why not?"

"She says she's not hungry. If you want my advice, you'll leave the poor lamb alone. I'll make her up something . . ."

"I'll do it," he grabbed an empty plate and started forking food on to it. Mrs Burchfield began to speak, but he interrupted angrily, "I said *I'll* take her some!"

Her mouth tightened. I suppose she had to take it, but I could practically feel her counting to ten. Or maybe fifty. If he'd spoken to me like that, I'd have socked him one with the soup ladle.

# 8

# Being sensible

He handed me a glass and the half-full bottle of water.

"I don't think I should come . . ." I began.

"Oh, come on, she does this all the time."

I followed him past the kitchen doorway. Mrs Burchfield watched us go. We came to a door. Peter elbowed it open.

Karen was sitting in the far corner, watching cartoons on a small portable TV. When the whole chair pivoted round with her, I realized that it was a wheelchair. She looked at me as if I was a terrifying monster with three heads.

"Say hello to Joanne," Peter said curtly.

"Hello."

My voice in reply sounded abnormally loud. Peter put the plate on her table, pushing aside coloured pencils and paper to make room. I added the glass and bottle. There was a drawing of clowns with bright purple pantaloons.

"Did you do these?"

She whispered, "Yes."

"They're very good," I tried another smile. This time there was a faint one in response.

"My mother's an artist," I told her.

"Oh," she whispered.

I had a mental picture of myself, turning stiff cards like the ones they use for skating competitions. I said something. She replied in one or two words. I turned over another card in my mind, groping for something to talk about.

Peter had turned his back on us, and was giving his undivided attention to Mr Magoo. For someone who despised TV, he did a good impression of an addict.

Karen picked at her food as if it might possibly explode if roughly prodded. Like Peter, she was very fair. She looked small for eight. Her hair was cut in a fringe and tied back in two old-fashioned plaits. Metal and plastic callipers grasped both her thin legs.

The cartoon ended. Peter noticed us again.

"D'you want dessert?"

Naturally, she shook her head. She laid down the knife and fork and stared at him. We left with the barely-touched plate. For two paper-clips, I'd have cheerfully smashed it over his ash-blonde head.

Our salad plates had been cleared. Two dishes of sorbet were sitting on the table, with a glass bowl of fresh fruit salad in the middle. The box with the bracelet still lay beside my dish.

I'd lost my appetite. It was time to say thank you and go, while I could still be polite.

He took a spoonful of sorbet. "Pineapple. I don't imagine she'll try it. Ridiculous child. She gets her own way all the time."

"It seems to run in the family."

"Meaning?"

I let him work it out.

"I'm sixteen, she's eight . . ." he said levelly.

". . . and you treat her as if she was about two."

"Is that so? What do you know about . . ."

"Or less than two. As if she had no feelings at all.

66

Taking me into her room like that, as if she was some kind of exhibit at a . . ."

"At what? A zoo? Is that what you think? That *was* the word you were thinking of?"

"No, I wasn't. Don't be stupid. She's only a . . ."

"She's a cripple," he said harshly. He dug the spoon deep into the sorbet. "Not a pretty word but, if it makes you feel better, I'll say it."

"I'm not talking about how *I* feel," my voice rose. "You're not listening to me. I'm talking about how *she* feels, when you treat her like that, as if she . . ."

"Don't tell me how to treat her. She's my sister. You know nothing about . . ."

"I know enough. It's *you*. You went in there like a bulldozer or something! It was so embarrassing! I didn't know what to say to her."

"Don't blame me if you feel inadequate."

I was on my feet, yelling that if anyone was inadequate around here it was him. I said he was more of a cripple than she was.

He stood up. His chair wavered a second, then toppled over, clattering loudly on to the tiles. He kicked it violently aside and went out through the door. I was shaking. I watched him go across the lawn and into the trees, slamming a low branch aside.

I was shaking, but I was glad I'd said it. Karen's bad legs weren't any kind of problem, compared to being stuck with a brother like Peter.

My stomach was still churning when I found the bike and began cycling down the drive. The breeze was cool on my face. The best of the day had gone. By the time I'd rounded the curve and got out of sight of the house, I could feel the first rapid spits of rain.

"Careful!"

I braked too late. My front wheel hit something. The bike keeled over with me sprawling under it.

I looked up. Larry the chauffeur in dark overalls, sleeves rolled. He was still wearing sun-glasses, though the sun had gone. He lifted the bike, and offered me a hand, but I struggled upright by myself.

"You hit the rake."

"I didn't see it."

"You weren't looking."

I could smell his hair cream, and sweat and earth.

"Can I have my bike, please."

"In a moment."

I stared at him. The sun-glasses hid his eyes.

"In a moment," he said again. "Once you stop shaking. Ride out on to the main road in that state, and you're liable to get yourself killed."

I looked fixedly at the gravel, willing my heart to slow its pounding. Rain darkened the grey stones. I brushed the hair from my eyes. As calmly as I could, I stretched out for the handlebar. He let go.

"Just as a matter of interest," he said, "do you usually cycle with your head down? Or has our Master Peter been upsetting you?"

I got astride my bike. To my horror he caught hold of the handlebar again.

"You look like a sensible girl, Miss Fletcher."

"Please," I said helplessly.

"Let's keep it that way," he went on. "Let's all be sensible. We don't want anyone getting hurt, do we?"

He smiled at me. Perfect teeth. Very white between the black of moustache and beard. All the better to eat you with . . .

He stepped aside. I pedalled down the rest of the drive, and out on to the main road, with my knuckles so tight on the grips that they were sore when I finally relaxed. The rain was plummeting before I reached the bridge.

What did he mean, "be sensible"? How would I get hurt? On the roads or some other way? He was horrible. Anyone who wore dark glasses in the rain had to be hiding something. No wonder Peter felt haunted. A brief shoot of sympathy for Peter raised its head above ground. I thought of Karen, and squashed it flat.

I saw Brian's car with a feeling of relief so intense it surprised me. He was at the kitchen table, reading his newspaper.

"Good grief, have you been in the river?"

I was soaked, but I couldn't help smiling. I was so glad he was home. He looked normal. Safe, predictable and normal.

"The sun was shining when I left." I squeezed the ends of my hair. Drips fell to the floor.

"Go and change."

"It's mostly my hair . . ."

"Change," he ordered. "And shower first. Suppose Anne phones and I have to say, no, she can't speak to you, she's got pneumonia."

He looked more tired than usual.

"How was your day?"

I felt strange asking. It was Mum's phrase.

"Hectic as usual. Please go and change. You're making me shiver."

"You look awfully tired."

Brian stood up, took off his reading glasses and peered at himself in the mirror.

"Perhaps I should see a friendly plastic surgeon. Do something about these bags. I gather it's getting less expensive."

"You wouldn't."

He laughed at my shocked face. "Don't get agitated.

69

They don't worry me that much. I'll have to learn how to grow old gracefully."

"You're not old."

"Say that again."

I paused in the doorway, struck by his tone.

"You're not old."

"I believe she means it."

I felt a sudden quiver, as if we were really talking to one another, the real me, to the real Brian, instead of skirting round one another, using words as if they were punting poles. In that moment, he wasn't a high-powered lawyer, but someone ordinary, who'd been a little boy once and would be an old man and would some day die.

"Would you put that in writing and sign it?"

"If you like."

"I like." He circled finger and thumb to sign OK. "You do that. I'll keep it in a gold frame on my desk, and read it at frequent intervals."

In the blissful warmth of the shower, I pondered it all. I couldn't think what it would be like to be past forty. Then I tried to imagine Brian as a little boy, to picture him with toy cars and a teddy bear. I laughed out loud. I'd conjured up a bespectacled Brian aged five. In dark grey pin-stripe shorts . . .

Later on, while we were eating, I remembered what Peter had said about seeing Brian in town at some restaurant. I was curious to know if it had been him, but I couldn't ask without explaining how I knew. I didn't want to do that. I didn't want to talk about Peter Niemenen. The meal over, Brian went off to the study and I came upstairs.

Later, when I switched the light off and turned to pray, I felt guilty, for the first time, about shouting at Peter. Not guilty exactly, just uneasy, so I prayed for him and his sister, asking that somehow he'd see beyond the wheelchair and the callipers. That he'd see a shy little girl with huge blue eyes who liked drawing purple clowns and deserved more than she was getting. I prayed that somehow Karen could learn not to be so afraid of him, because I thought that probably made him worse. But I didn't know how either thing could happen.

I thought about the bracelet. What would he do with it? The stones had looked like turquoise. I didn't have anything like it in my motley collection of jewellery. Then I remembered Neil Campbell's Christmas sardine tin, lying in the dressing-table drawer. Just my luck. My friends gave me sardines. People I didn't like bought me silver bracelets.

After that I prayed for Mum, that she'd really enjoy herself and have no problems and come home safe. Then I got a bit carried away with myself and prayed for Brian. It felt like trying shoes on the wrong feet. Still, I decided, tonight had been an improvement. I had to try harder to like him. If I worked at it, things might improve even more.

# 9

# Between the cartoons

The following day Brian worked at home. I messed about in the workshop, reading back numbers of *Arts Monthly*. Then at lunchtime he announced that he'd done all he wanted to.

"Let's have lunch in the village, at the Black Bull. I've an appointment in Chiddlebury this afternoon. If you want to come, you could amuse yourself wandering round the shops for an hour or so."

"I could look for sandals."

"Right. Get your glad rags on. We'll go and sample Mrs Norman's apple pie."

Remembering my resolve to try harder, I changed into the white dress. I had a pale blue denim jacket that looked all right on top of it.

The Black Bull wasn't busy — some middle-aged touristy-looking couples, a few local folk, and one family with small children. The youngest, a boy of about three in a Batman T-shirt, was more interested in getting the horseshoes off the wall than eating his cheese roll.

"This really is excellent," Brian waved a spoonful of apple pie at me. "You ought to have some."

"I couldn't. I'm full to bursting."

"What a very uncouth expression. I was brought up

to call it an 'elegant sufficiency'." He added more cream. "I doubt if Anne will be eating better than this. In my experience, the excellence or otherwise of French cookery, especially in Paris, depends largely on the prevailing mood of the chef."

"D'you like Italian food?"

It was as if some mischievous spirit put the words in my mouth.

"Now and then. Why?" He gave his mouth a quick dab with the napkin.

"I just wondered."

I went on. Like picking at a spot. You know it's wrong but you can't stop.

"One of the girls at school said there was a good place in town."

"Did she?"

"It's in Hanover Street."

"Well, I think I'm ready for coffee."

Brian twisted round to catch Mrs Norman's eye. I felt as if I'd been caught shoplifting. Peter *couldn't* have seen him. It must have been someone else in the restaurant.

Across from us, the older boy, cowboy hat slung round his neck, had reached the bottom of his orange juice and was making revolting noises through the straw. His mother was vainly trying to get the toddler to come out from under the table. The father was staring at a glass of cider. You got the feeling it had already been a long day.

Brian had bought a newspaper at the Post Office on the way in. He unfolded it while he waited for coffee, to study the cricket scores. Facing me were the headlines, "Moscow admits two killed in Karelia Crisis" and "Fresh riots in Petrozavodsk".

Suddenly I thought of Mum, and how she'd joked

about missing the riots in Paris twenty years before. A little shiver ran up my spine. I read down the article. Paris wasn't mentioned, but they were linking the riots in Karelia with demonstrations by exiled Karelian nationalists in New York, where some big Russian delegation was over for something. Brian moved the paper before I got it all.

"Oh, sorry. Were you reading something?"

"It's that thing that was on TV the other night. The stone-throwing in New York. Mum was joking about it."

He raised an eyebrow.

"You're not worrying about her . . ."

I bit my lip. She hadn't phoned us apart from when she first arrived, but that didn't mean anything. We knew she'd be busy.

"New York is quite a long way from Paris, or it was when I did geography. They don't mention Paris, do they?"

He turned the paper round and scanned the article for a few moments. "These aren't international terrorists," he tapped the page. "And they're not very organized either. As far as I can gather," he went on, "this is a small nationalist minority trying to put some pressure on the government in Moscow. In a way, it's bound to . . ."

Before he could finish, we had company. Unwelcome company. Hesitant, terribly polite, nauseatingly well-mannered.

"Good morning, sir. I thought it might be you. Recognized you through the window. And the car, of course."

Brian was slightly taken aback. He'd only spoken to Peter once, for five minutes. Mild surprise in his eyes, therefore, at the warmth of dear Peter's dazzling smile.

Watching what followed, gradually it dawned on me that Brian was flattered. Incredibly, he felt honoured that Peter had come in to speak to us. He didn't know I'd been to lunch and left in disgust. He didn't know that this son of a famous man was, beneath the shining exterior, a pain in the neck. And it was too late to wise him up . . .

Besides, Brian recognized another public school boy when he saw one. He fell for the act like a true sucker. How exactly Peter managed it, I don't know. It was like a conjuring trick. One minute he was wavering beside the table like a hesitant stork, the next he was having coffee with us, talking about Brian's Mercedes, about turbo-chargers and car-phones, "sirring" Brian left, right and centre.

Each time my glare caught his eye, he put on a hurt, puzzled look. My hands itched to pick up the sugar bowl and empty it down his neck. Instead I tried being subtle.

"Brian, shouldn't we be going soon?"

"My word, is that the time?" He turned to Peter, "Sorry, we can't linger. Shopping expedition in Chiddlebury."

Oh? Chiddlebury? Were we? Then would we . . . of course it might seem terribly intrusive . . . hate to impose, sir . . . but would Brian mind terribly, sir, if he took advantage and cadged a lift? Useful to get to the bank, sir.

Good old sir said it was fine with him. Sir's step-daughter reached fizzing point.

Brian went to settle the bill.

"What are you playing at?" I hissed angrily.

"Getting you hot and bothered? I like the dress by the way. Very chic."

"You don't need to go to a bank."

"Yes I do and I'll tell you why if you like."

"I don't like."

"Could you be angry more quietly? People are beginning to look our way . . ."

One or two heads were indeed turning. I took a deep breath. "Before my step-father comes back, you are going to develop a sudden headache and leave."

"I apologize for yesterday."

"A migraine. Pleurisy even."

"I'm sorry."

"You ought to be."

"Give me a chance," he urged. "Look, something's happened, something important. I'll tell you about it if you stop snapping at me."

"I'm not snapping. I just want you to think of somewhere else you'd rather be."

"I said I was sorry. I'll grovel on the carpet if you want me to."

I thought he just might do it.

"So what happened?" I said grudgingly.

"You're not going to believe me," he said slowly.

"Try me."

"Before I went to bed last night I . . ."

"Right then, everyone ready?"

Peter fell silent as Brian came up. We went out to the car. Peter tried most politely to get Brian to take the money for his coffee. Brian just as politely would have none of it. It was all awfully, awfully civilized. I sat in the back, seething, wondering what game Peter was playing now. I trusted him about as far as I could throw one of Mr Wilson's cows. What had happened before he went to bed? Had he wrestled with a burglar? Brushed his teeth with shoe polish?

When we reached Chiddlebury, Brian went off to see his client. Some architect whose sheltered houses were falling down, he told us. We were to meet back at the car at four.

Chiddlebury wasn't big. It had a market on Thursdays, and a few interesting shops, but tourists came to see the remains of the medieval castle, so the square was crowded with cars and coaches.

The weather couldn't make its mind up, but a few optimists were wearing sun-hats. I'd abandoned the idea of looking for new sandals, and I waited on a seat beside the War Memorial while Peter went to the bank.

Well, I told myself, at least he apologized. Maybe he's not a complete pain. I wondered what exactly had happened the previous night, the thing he said I wouldn't believe. Maybe he'd apologized to his sister too. That could be it. I felt a bit guilty. I'd been too mean to let him tell me.

He emerged from the bank, saw me and gave a quick wave, then began dodging his way across the busy road. He could have been a student on holiday from Germany or Scandinavia. He certainly didn't look British.

"Sorry. Big queue. Like an ice-cream?"

"I've just had a huge lunch," I told him.

"Come on, I'll pay."

"Is that what you needed money for? Buying ice-cream?"

"Well, I've tried using beads but they throw them back at me."

It was meant as a joke. Out in the air between us, it took on another meaning. We each knew what the other was thinking. Only it had been a bracelet, not beads.

"I'll have an ice-cream if you . . ." I began hurriedly.

"Maybe it's too soon after your . . ."

We both smiled. The tension lessened a fraction.

"What do you want to do?" he asked.

"Nothing specially."

He glanced at his wrist.

"I have to make a phone call, but I can do it later. Ever seen the castle?"

I hadn't. He bought two ice-creams, and we licked our way round to the ruins. He told me a bit about the history of the place as we walked. Once or twice when I glanced at him, I got the feeling that there *was* something wrong, that something had happened to worry or excite him. But I didn't like to ask. If he wanted me to know he'd have to tell me.

We leaned on the upper wall. The grey stones were warm. Below us the ancient moat was swathed in bright grass, freshly cut. On the gravel path a group of chattering Koreans were photographing one another.

"What do they do with all the prints? They must take hundreds."

"Take them home. Show them off to all the relatives."

He turned, elbows on the wall, face to the sun. "You don't have any brothers or sisters, do you?"

"No."

"Does it bother you?"

"Not specially. I don't go about thinking, oh dear, I'm an only child, or anything, if that's what you mean."

"I was on my own for eight years," he said. "I mean, until Karen was born."

"Were you at home?"

I meant had he started boarding school, but he took it another way.

"No. We were all in Boston because Father was

doing concerts. The hotel had a pool on the roof. One of the attendants taught me to dive. He had muscles like a weight-lifter, and a snake tattoo on one arm, right here. He could make it move."

He turned back round. The Koreans had finished with the moat and were going towards the staircase that led to our level.

He said suddenly, "If she'd been born today, she'd have been killed."

"Who would?"

"My sister."

He glanced at me, then shrugged.

"Don't look so shocked. Doctors do it every day."

"That's not true . . ."

"Of course it's true. They sedate them so they won't cry, and starve them to death."

"You're sick." My voice was thick with disgust.

"Am I? I'm just telling you what happens. *I* don't do it. It's the people in the white coats that do it."

I couldn't argue. I didn't know whether he was telling the truth or not. I'd never thought about it. But I had to fight back.

"I don't believe you. You can't mean she'd be better dead!"

"I didn't say that . . ."

The Koreans had arrived beside us and were exclaiming over the view of the town.

"Let's move," Peter said abruptly.

We walked along the parapet, down the steps, and under the dark arching stonework to the moat. We were almost back round at the entrance gate when he stopped beside a vacant bench.

"You might as well hear it all," he said.

I sat on the bench. He squatted on the grass and told me about Karen. She had spina bifida. When she was born, she'd had a huge head, hydro-something he called it. She looked normal now, and there was nothing wrong with her mind, so she went to an ordinary school in the next village. But she still had a tube inside her. If it got infected, he said, she could die. And she'd never walk properly.

The strong sweet smell of new-cut grass hung in the air. I couldn't think of anything to say. Then I was glad I'd kept my big mouth shut, because it seemed that once he'd started, he wanted to talk about everything.

He began to tell me about his mother. Three days after the birth, she'd walked out of the hospital and into the highway. The truck driver thought at first she was a white bag blown into the road, billowing in the evening breeze.

"How can you remember . . . ?" I faltered.

"What the man said?"

I nodded, hardly trusting myself to speak. For I could see it. The traffic roaring past in the rush hour, and his mother, wandering out on to the road, tossed into the air . . .

"They put it on TV. Famous man's wife, you see. It was a news bulletin between the cartoons. Donald Duck."

I stared at him.

"But didn't they . . . Didn't you know before . . . ?"

"They were waiting for my father to come home and tell me. And they waited for the concert interval before they told *him*."

"But he came home then?"

He didn't hear me. Time had slipped. He was back in a darkened room with his childhood ending and only a talking Technicolor Duck for company.

I tried to remember how I'd felt when Dad died. It was too far away. I'd been only five. I remembered

80

being left with a neighbour, and playing with her black-and-white collie dog in front of the fire. But, looking back, it was the feel of the dog's warm smooth coat I remembered, not how I'd felt when Mum had said Dad wouldn't be coming home. I couldn't even remember whether I'd cried or not.

I looked at Peter's bowed head and felt incredibly sorry for him. Incredibly helpless too. He needed God so much. He needed to know Jesus, and all the comfort and security that faith would give him. Because there was one thing I could remember — the emptiness I used to feel in the night sometimes, before I knew that there was a God and that he loved me.

It was all so simple, and so important, but I didn't know how to begin to tell Peter.

He got to his feet, brushing grass off his trousers. Brushing away the past. I had to speak. Even if I messed it up.

"Peter, why did you think I wouldn't believe you?" I began hesitantly.

"Sorry?"

"At the Bull, you said it was important, but that I wouldn't believe you."

He looked puzzled.

"But I'm glad you've told me all this," I went on. "I don't know if you've ever . . ."

"Oh, that wasn't what I meant," he said quickly. He glanced at his watch. "I want to make a phone call. I was going to send a Swiftair letter in the village. Then when Tarzan said you were coming here, I realized I could phone. What's the matter?"

"I saw at least four telephones in your house," I said lamely.

"But they won't do. Not safe, you see . . ."

"Not what?"

"Because I've got father's New York hotel phone number in my diary." He tapped the hip pocket of his denims. "When Tarzan said Chiddlebury, inspiration hit my weary brain like a burst of neon light, because they've got those new boxes here. If I send it from here, Larry won't know about it."

"You're confusing me. Why does that matter?"

He offered his hand to help me up.

"Why isn't Larry to know?"

"Because it's about him. Because I found a gun in his room last night. In a little brown case under his bed, complete with all the dinky little parts."

"I don't believe you!"

"There you are. That's exactly what I thought you'd say."

# 10
# Breaking point

"You can't telephone America." I couldn't believe he was serious.

"Of course you can. All you need is a phone card or a stack of one pound coins. And I've got his hotel number. I'll leave a message for him. 'Dearest Pa, new chauffeur has Smith and Wesson, suspect criminal intent. Please advise.' Exciting, isn't it? Like one of those *Untouchables* films."

We were passing through the exit from the castle grounds. He imitated a gangster machine-gunning the information board, and the people waiting to pay at the window smiled indulgently.

"Peter, you can't do this. He's probably got a licence for it. All you'll do is cause trouble . . ."

"Lots and lots," he smiled cheerfully. "If it was a hunting rifle, fair enough, but a pistol? Don't frown at me like that. It's a kind of scientific experiment. Or like Bonfire Night. Light fuse, stand well back, see the pretty colours go whoosh in the sky."

It was his sanity that had gone whoosh. His sanity and my peace of mind.

"Peter, if this is true, you've got to tell the police."

"No, I'm telling Father first."

"Why? He's too far away to do anything. And

what were you doing in Larry's room anyway?" I asked.

He ignored me. We reached the phone boxes, and he pulled a long tube of one pound coins from his pocket. He set them on the ledge inside and checked a small address book. Again I tried to get him to change his mind. He made faces at me through the door.

I gave up. Slowly I made my way along the street, looking in windows. There were piles of cheeses in Hutchison the Dairy: yellow Cheddar and red-coated Edam, cylinders of soft cheese coated with herbs. Pathetic red-mouthed rabbits hung upside down in the butcher's. The newsagent's offered cheap china ornaments, plastic soldiers, water-pistols and sun-bleached paperbacks.

My mind was reeling. Suppose the gruesome Larry did have a gun? I didn't like the idea much. But if he was up to no good, why was he trimming hedges and mending fences? On the other hand, how did I know Peter was telling the truth? He could easily have invented the whole thing. His moods changed so fast, it made me unsure how much of anything he said was the truth.

What he'd told me about his mother sounded true. I had seen Karen with my own eyes. Maybe all the rest was true. It was so hard to know. Keeping up with Peter was like trying to stand upright on rolling logs in a moving river.

There was a church across the road, a low modern building set back from the pavement, as if it had snuggled itself into a gap in the old terrace. I crossed to read the notice board.

There were lots of things happening, including a youth club barbecue the following Saturday. Big deal. I couldn't go on my own. While we'd all been living in our old house in the city, I'd gone to the local church. A couple of my friends from school had even come with me a few times. Just when I was getting to know people there, we'd moved. And I never saw my old friends after school now because we lived so far out of town.

Lord, I complained, this isn't fair. I really need someone to talk to. Couldn't you have given me somebody normal for a neighbour? Then I saw Peter on the other side of the street. He waved.

Lord Jesus, I breathed, I'm sorry. I know he needs you but, honestly, I can't do it. I'm sorry about his mother and Karen, but it's too hard. I know it's a rotten thing to say, but I've had enough of him.

Peter looked pleased with himself as he crossed over.

"The wonders of British Telecom. Got through first time."

He glanced at the board.

"Thinking of signing on? Bit young for the Senior Citizens' Friendship Circle, I suppose. Breaking of Bread, Sunday evening. That sounds exciting. Kind of like a tug of war."

"It means Holy Communion."

"Wholly humbug."

"Say that again?"

"Humbug. Hypocrisy. Rubbish."

I was suddenly very calm, not flustered at all.

"It's not rubbish. Jesus dying on the cross was the most important thing that's ever happened."

He looked steadily at me.

"I've got it," he exclaimed. "You're a nun in disguise."

"I just happen to believe in God. You don't, I suppose."

"Why should I? What's God ever done for me?

85

Nothing. Except maybe mess up my life. If there is a God." He glanced back at the notice board. I opened my mouth to speak, but he went on harshly, "If it makes you happy, I'm happy for you. Just don't let's waste the day talking about it, OK?

His sudden bitterness hurt me.

"*You* don't need God to mess up your life, Peter."

"What's that supposed to mean?"

"Oh, nothing," I said after a second or two. "Forget it."

It had been a petty thing to say. I didn't really want to argue with him. He didn't know what he was talking about. I'd been like that a year before, and I knew arguing wouldn't help. We stood there in silence for a few moments.

"It's nearly four," I said eventually. "We ought to get back to the car."

He was staring at the ground.

"Brian might be there already. We ought to be getting back."

"All the things we ought to do," he said slowly, raising his head. "They never admit it in Physics," he looked at me, "but Oughts have to be the heaviest things in the universe."

I hadn't a clue what he was talking about, except that it sounded kind of sad. On the way back to the car park he said he was thirsty, was I? I said yes, basically to show I wasn't mad at him, and he bought two chilled cans of orange from a kiosk. We came to a tiny art-gallery place. I stopped for a quick look at the window.

"Your mother's an artist, isn't she? I heard you telling Karen."

"There's nothing of hers here. She uses a gallery in town."

"What kind of things does she do?"

"Oils mostly. Right now she's into room interiors, with or without people. But for some reason she thinks she's in a rut. That's why she was keen on this teaching thing in France."

"Does she do animals?"

"I don't think she's ever tried. Why?"

"I was thinking of Tequila," he explained. "She's the best horse I've had. I wouldn't mind a picture of her."

"I could ask," I began. "I don't think she's ever painted a horse but I suppose she . . ."

"There's the boss," Peter interrupted.

Brian was striding along past the chemist's on the other side of the street. He hadn't seen us. We began walking.

"Keeps himself pretty fit, doesn't he?" Peter commented. "That day at the bridge, he came hurtling along the road as if . . ."

"Did you really think it was the horse that scared me? Because it wasn't. Putting on that stupid voice, trying to sell me your watch. I thought you were a tramp."

"What do you mean? Those were my best jeans."

"You were filthy. You looked as if you'd been *sleeping* in a ditch, not just . . . What's wrong?"

He'd stopped abruptly. Following the line of his eye, I saw for myself what was wrong.

Larry.

He was beside Brian's car, waiting for us. Black T-shirt, with sleeves rolled up above the elbows, dark glasses in place. He was leaning on the Mercedes bonnet, arms folded. He hadn't seen us. A quick glance confirmed that Brian had seen him.

"You'd better get over there fast!" I exclaimed.

"What for? They both speak English."

"Listen, Brian's paranoid about that car. He'll go crazy if there's a scratch half a centimetre long. Don't just stand there, do something, Peter!"

"Like what? Rush over and get caught in the middle when they start slugging one another?"

Larry straightened up and replied to whatever Brian had said.

"Why is he here?"

"Maybe they told him at the Bull that I was with you," Peter suggested. "Tarzan told Mrs Norman we were coming here, remember? At the door."

"I meant, why has he bothered? Did you mess up his things before you left or something?"

Peter made a face. He tried to sound casual.

"He makes this big thing of having to know where I am if I leave the village. The man's a creep. He's up to something. And I bet he doesn't have a gun licence . . . Here we go," his voice rose, "they've spotted us."

They had. We had no choice but to cross over.

Brian was seething. He spoke to Peter so politely it frightened me more than if he'd shouted. "Perhaps you would kindly assure this *gentleman*" (a slight hesitation) "that you accompanied us here entirely of your own free will. He appears to think my purposes were nefarious in the extreme."

I hoped Peter knew what that meant, because I didn't.

Peter confirmed that he'd asked for a lift.

Larry's mouth was set in a tight angry line.

"So what's wrong with your father's car?"

"With the car? Nothing. The car I like."

Larry chose to ignore the insult.

"Fine. So next time, use it. That's what I'm for.

Unless maybe you think I have nothing better to do than hunt for you all round the county."

Peter made a very rude suggestion as to what he might better do. Brian suddenly remembered he had an innocent child to protect, and ordered me into the car. I looked at him, and decided not to argue.

I shrank low into the seat, and closed my eyes, coward that I was. A moment later, Brian got in himself and started the engine.

"Who is that character?"

"Peter? He's Carl Niemenen's son, you met him your . . ."

"Mephistopheles with the muscles."

He could only mean Larry.

"He's their chauffeur. Really, he is," I added as Brian snorted in disbelief. He edged the car into the main road. I couldn't see where Peter and Larry had gone.

"I've a good mind to call on his employer," he said angrily.

"He's in New York. Peter told me."

There was another humph of irritation.

We drove the rest of the way home in uneasy silence.

As we came in through the kitchen door, the phone was ringing. I lifted it, listened, then held it out for Brian.

"Who is it?" he said.

"She didn't say."

But I thought I'd recognized the voice. It sounded like the woman I'd seen in the office. The woman who'd looked right through me, Mrs Delaney. I saw again her high heels and red finger-nails. Brian took the phone, turning his back on me.

I switched on the radio, and he barked at me with

one hand over the receiver, couldn't I see he was on the phone?

So I turned off the radio and sat down till the kettle would boil.

"Do you mind?"

"Do I mind what?"

He made a brushing movement with his hand, meaning that I should go elsewhere.

I could do nothing right. I was safer out of his way. I decided to wash my hair in the shower. While I was drying it upstairs, thinking about the afternoon and wondering how Peter was surviving, I put on a tape. A few seconds later, Brian came to the foot of the stairs and yelled at me to turn down the volume. Either his feathers were still ruffled after the encounter with Larry, or else it was the phone call.

Why was she phoning him at home? I didn't like it. He practically never got phone calls at home from clients. I wished now that I'd asked Peter to describe the woman he'd seen at the restaurant. A grubby, horrible suspicion had begun to scrabble at the back of my mind on that first day when he'd been so certain it was Brian. I'd squashed it, but now it was taking shape again, and beginning to wriggle like something dark at the bottom of a pond.

Brian yelled up at me later to say the food was on the table. It was shepherd's pie, ready-baked for the microwave, one of those complete meals that looks better on the packet. I didn't talk. He was still in a bad mood. I was being a good girl. So it took me by surprise when he tossed a verbal grenade into the gravy.

"I'd rather you didn't get too friendly with the Niemenen boy."

I looked at him blankly.

"After what happened today, I've decided I don't want you to have anything to do with him, particularly while Anne's away."

"Why not?"

It wasn't meant to sound cheeky, but he took it that way.

"Never mind why not. You're to have nothing to do with him. I made one error of judgment today, and I'm not going to make another."

"I didn't want him to come," I protested.

"Then you might have given me some indication of that."

That annoyed me, considering what he'd been like at the Bull. He was being pompous and silly.

"So what have I to do? Wear a veil round the village, in case he recognizes me and says hello?"

"Don't be ridiculous."

"I'm not being ridiculous. I won't see any of my friends till September, and there's no one in this village my age . . ."

"That's beside the point . . ."

"I mean, there's his sister, but she's only eight and she's too terrified to talk to me."

"What do you mean she's terrified? Where did you meet her?"

"When I went for lunch," I said reluctantly.

"Went for lunch where?"

"To their house. Yesterday."

"I see. And is there anything else I've not been informed of?"

His tone really riled me. Like a fussy teacher being sarcastic over a missing rubber.

"I didn't realize I had to ask for permission."

"Don't be pert with me, madam."

"I'm not five you know. I'm fifteen!"

"I'm well aware of that. If you were five you'd be a heck of a lot easier to live with!"

I stood up, pushing away my plate.

"Where d'you think you're going?"

"Anywhere away from you!"

I didn't care what I said. My self-control was breaking like the last strands of a stretched rope.

He began to speak but I talked louder.

"And, anyway, why's it so wrong for me to have lunch with Peter? Karen was there too, and Mrs Burchfield. Just because it's his house? What's so terrible about that? I suppose if he'd taken me to an expensive restaurant in the town that would have been all right."

"What precisely does that mean?"

"You work it out! Peter saw you!"

He stood up. I moved, so that the table was between us.

"God deliver me from hysterical teenagers!"

"Don't bring God into it . . ."

"No, that's your speciality, isn't it? You've more or less cornered the market in piety, haven't you? I'm surprised we don't have a grotto in the garden with plaster . . ."

"I hate you," I yelled. "I wish my mother had never laid eyes on you! You've got her, with your money and your big car and your smooth talk, but you haven't got me!"

I was shaking with rage.

The muscles twitched in his jaw. I thought he was going to lean across and hit me.

He used words instead.

"Get out of my sight."

I fled from the kitchen, blind, hot, head throbbing.

Through the sitting-room, through the French windows to the garden, and then to the road. I slowed down at the edge of the barley field, and walked the length of it to the stile. Through clenched teeth I repeated how much I hated Brian, and how desperately unfair and dreadful life was. Angrily, I asked God if he had any idea what he was doing to me. There couldn't have been a bird left within half a mile by the time my sobbing eased.

# 11
# Out of control

I didn't come back till the evening breeze began to make me shiver. I meant to go upstairs, but Brian saw me coming.

He slid the French windows open wide. I went into the room, not looking at him. The last thing I wanted to do was talk.

"Joanne."

I stopped. Didn't turn.

"Your friend Mrs Campbell phoned."

"Oh."

"To confirm about the keys. I don't know what arrangement Anne has made with Betty, so I informed her you would find out and telephone them in the morning."

It didn't surprise me that I'd missed that phone call. Just one more inevitable bit of misery.

"Joanne, wait a moment, please."

Reluctantly I turned round. Seeing the glass in his hand, my hatred of him curled into a tighter ball.

"Contrary to what you may suppose, I realize this hasn't been an easy year for you," he studied the clear liquid, then looked at me.

"Nor has it been easy for me. Perhaps that wouldn't occur to you."

Where was this leading? I studied the carpet, wishing he would be done.

"Obviously not. Well, you might think it over. Sometimes in this life, if something's going to work, it requires a certain amount of compromise." He sipped at the glass. I thought he'd said all he wanted to, but there was more. "Of course, the ability to make mutual concessions is an acquired skill, not an inherent one. Everyone instinctively wants to be the centre of the universe. Unfortunately, we only appear to have one planet at our disposal."

"Can I go now?"

He ran a finger slowly backwards and forwards on the rim of the glass.

"A curious arrangement, don't you think? Infinite galaxies out there, and all of us crammed together down here. Curious. Of course you can go." His voice changed abruptly. "I don't suppose for a moment that anything I've said has made the slightest impression on your implacable self-esteem."

With that he turned his back, put the glass down and pressed the TV into life.

Upstairs I lay for ages, shuffling anger and bitterness in my mind like a pack of grubby cards. Above me the roof was creaking and shifting. The weather was changing. When I went to close the window, a dark shape swooped down towards the far hedge. It could have been an owl. I watched for a while, but didn't see it again. The half moon was blurred by clouds.

I closed the curtains, and got back into bed. I couldn't stop being me, if that was what Brian meant. Nobody could stop being the person they were. What did he want me to be? Something transparent like a blob of jelly, with no personality at all? The real truth was that he wanted everyone to dance round him.

If anyone acted as if he was the centre of the universe, it was Brian. He hadn't a clue how I felt about anything. Not a clue. All that he wanted was for me to merge into the background, a decorative detail in a good dress. He wanted me to fit round his ideas, round his marriage with my mother.

All that bilge about compromise and mutual concessions. Good grief, what kind of compromise did he think he'd made? Swapping his two-seater Porsche for the family-size Mercedes?

My thoughts wandered distractedly over all that had happened since the day began. I thought about Peter. How he was sad and funny and bitter all at once. And maybe a bit crazy too. I wondered what his father would make of the message, and if Larry really did have a gun. Would I see him again? Would I go against Brian or not?

I thought about Mum, wondering if she was finding her lost youth, or whatever France was supposed to give her. I missed her. But I wanted her back the way she'd been before Brian. So wanting her was pointless. Five days till she was due home.

I thought of the Campbells coming to our empty house, and wished I could somehow stay on with them. I could talk to them about things Mum and Brian would never understand.

What if the Campbells didn't want you to stay? said a voice in my head. What if they've had enough of you?

I turned the pillow to the cool side. They would want me. They liked me. Not just the twins. Mr and Mrs Campbell liked me too.

Are you sure? The voice in my head persisted.

Maybe you only think they like you. People change. A year is a long time. Why should they like you? You think two weeks with them gives you some sort of status? And you're supposed to be a Christian. That's what you told them. That's a joke. If they could see what you were really like, they'd not want to know you. Because you're a wash-out at that too. Face it. You don't matter that much, to them or anyone.

The voice won.

I couldn't find any words to pray with. God wouldn't hear my pathetic attempts. So much for Brian's little theory, I thought bitterly. I couldn't have felt less like the centre of the universe. As far as I could see, it wouldn't have made any difference to anybody if I'd never been born.

Next morning, I was woken by Betty's knock on the bedroom door.

"You awake, pet? I've brought some tea up. Five minutes to ten," she added cheerfully, handing me a mug. "Time you had something in your tummy if you don't want a headache. I'll take your washing. We might be lucky. There's a nice breeze if the rain keeps off."

Off she bustled with my dirty clothes. She clumped downstairs singing, "If you were the only girl in the world". When she got to the high bits in the verse, she dropped an octave.

She was spraying and polishing the inside of the kitchen window when I came down. I sneezed.

"Not catching a cold, I hope," she eyed me kindly.

"It's just the spray."

"Can't have you getting a cold, right at the start of your nice holidays. Here, before it goes out of my head again, your Dad's forgotten his house keys."

She drew them out of her apron pocket. "You'd better let him know, else he'll think he's dropped them in town."

I thawed a frozen roll, buttered it, and took it with a glass of milk to the sitting-room to phone the office. Life was so simple for Betty. School holidays were nice. Colds were the only enemy. Eat regularly to avoid headaches.

Chloe answered my call.

"Hi there. No, I don't think he's here. Hold on . . ." her voice disappeared then she came back.

"No, he's definitely not in his office. What's the problem?"

I explained about the keys. Someone was talking in the background, then Chloe spoke again.

"Miss Miller says he phoned to say he was working at home today."

"But he's not. The car's gone."

"P'raps he got half-way here, missed his keys and turned back," she suggested helpfully. "Wait a bit," she put her hand over the receiver again. "Sorry about that," she went on. "She says he seemed to be in a call box, so I expect that's what's happened."

I said I supposed it was.

"Listen. When he does get back," Chloe added, "would you tell him about old Mr Davis? You know, our car park man? He's had a heart attack. Mr Taylor found him. They've taken him to the Royal. Mr Barnes-Ingram's always been so good to him, I expect he'll want to know right away."

I asked how bad he was.

"We don't know yet. Miss Miller's trying to get in touch with his relatives. I expect she'll phone the hospital later."

I said I'd tell Brian as soon as he came in, and Chloe

said she'd phone if they got any word from the hospital.

Betty finished work at around twelve as usual. She came into the sitting-room to say goodbye, and to remind me to bring in the washing if the rain came on.

I was watching an old black-and-white film.

"Bette Davis? Bless me, that was an old film when *I* was a girl. You should be out getting fresh air, blow away the germs," she chided.

I said I'd go out once Brian came back. She took my remark at face value. In her world you said what you meant. Things stayed where you put them. Fresh air blew away germs. Feelings and emotions all had their own place, with a plastic bag round them to keep out the dust.

When the film finished, I had a bacon sandwich and coffee, and wandered over to the outhouse. The smells of paint, linseed oil and crayon dust were vaguely comforting. I read through some old copies of *Arts Monthly* then decided to do a pastel still life. A few apples from the fruit bowl, a white jug, a battered brass candle holder with two inches of green candle and three green marbles from Mum's box of useful bits and pieces.

I looked out once or twice to see if there was any sign of Brian, then I began enjoying what I was doing and forgot him. When my stomach said it was food time, I went back to the house, and saw to my surprise that it was well after six.

On the wall board, Mum had chalked, *Thursday: vegetarian lasagne. Cook from frozen. Mousse (thaw slightly)*.

I put the frozen lasagne into the oven and took two tubs of strawberry mousse out as instructed. But by the time it was all ready, there was still no sign of

Brian. I had mine on a tray in front of an excruciatingly stupid quiz game. By half past seven, I was uneasy, wondering if he'd had an accident with the car. I couldn't understand why he hadn't telephoned.

The rain finally came, and I dashed out to rescue Betty's good work, straining to see if there was any sign of the car in the distance. There wasn't.

By nine, the rain had stopped and I was feeling very uneasy. If he'd gone out feeling hung-over he could easily have crashed the car. I wondered if I should call the local police. I was trying to find the number when the phone rang. Relieved, I pounced on it.

"Where are you?" I said.

"At home, where should I be?"

"Oh, it's you."

"Well, I think it's me. Should I look in a mirror and check?"

"Don't bother. Goodnight, Peter."

"Hey, hold on. Who was I supposed to be?"

I explained about Brian.

He laughed, saying I sounded like a distracted mother hen.

"Listen," he went on, "I was going to take Tequila out now that the rain's stopped. Down by the river, I thought. We could meet at the bridge."

"I can't leave the house. Brian forgot his door keys this morning. And, anyway, I'm not supposed to have anything to do with you."

"We have interference on sound, lieutenant. Say that again?"

I gave him a strictly edited account of what Brian had said.

"But if he's not home, he's not going to know what you're doing."

"I just don't feel like another bawling out."

"Lost his temper, did he? Over *me*? Wow, that's encouraging. I didn't realize I . . ."

"Peter," I interrupted his ego trip, remembering what I'd wanted to ask. "Remember you thought you saw Brian with a woman, at a restaurant? What did she look like?"

He thought for a moment.

"Black hair, very posh red suit. High heels to match. And it definitely *was* Brian, in case you think I didn't recognize him. Why're you asking?"

"It doesn't matter."

He didn't speak right away.

"Hey, you can't fool your Uncle Peter," he said slowly. "Your imagination's gone into overdrive, hasn't it? You want me to phone the Campagnola and see if they've booked a table? He's probably telling her his step-daughter doesn't understand him . . ."

I slammed the phone down. Seconds later it rang again. I ignored it. Peter's fatuous comments were more than I could take. He was right about my imagination. It was out of control, like a bike without brakes. Yet even supposing he was right, and that Brian *was* somewhere with Mrs Delaney . . . He would have let me know. Or would he, after last night's row?

His filing cabinet was locked, but the key was in the desk drawer. I found a Mr Delaney in a card file. I took it to the kitchen and ate some chocolate biscuits, wondering if I was getting as crazy as Peter. Maybe there was something in the water supply.

I had to be crazy. What was I going to say when she answered the phone — "Could I have my step-father back please?"

I dialled the number.

A woman answered. Somebody foreign, perhaps Spanish, who said Meeses Delanee is not at zees address. I stammered that it was in the phone book. She was so sorry, did I want Meester Delanee? Could she tell me Mrs Delaney's number then? One moment. There was music in the background, and other voices, then a man's voice asked curtly what he could do for me.

I was already kicking myself, remembering that she was divorcing her husband. It was hardly likely that they lived in the same house any more.

I apologized for not having the right number. He didn't ask who I was, just gave me another phone number. When I hung up, I was sweating.

I dialled the new number. I had to be out of my head. Twenty times it rang. No one in. I began to feel light-headed. I was like a gambler down to his shirt and getting desperate. I had to phone someone. Who else could I try? The Campagnola, as Peter suggested? Even in my ragged state, that felt like the outer edge of ridiculous. I had to pull myself together.

I was staring out at the main road, across the fields, willing headlights to turn on to our road, when the phone shrilled again into the silence.

If it was Peter, I didn't want to speak to him, but it could be Brian, broken down somewhere, or in trouble (or at Mrs Delaney's, a voice whispered). It might even be Mum phoning from France . . .

"Hello?" I said cautiously.

"Good evening, this is Tobermory Tourist Office. Are you the lady that was enquiring about the haggis-hunting expedition?"

My mind went blank. Haggis hunting? Tobermory?

"Joanne, that *is* you, isn't it? It's me, Neil Campbell."

"Neil?" I said hesitantly, "Is that you? Your voice sounds funny."

"Oh. Well, it broke."

"Broke?" I echoed stupidly, before I realized what he meant.

"Listen, what happened to the phone call? You were supposed to let us know the arrangements for next week. Well, listen. Mum thinks it might be nearer eight before we get to your place. Dad wants to stop for lunch with some old naval buddy of his, so can you let your key-lady know, in case she goes out? Right, that's the official part. How are things with you?"

"Not bad," I lied.

He talked about what they'd been doing. He launched into a long tale about how Roddy had lost one of his new contact lenses on the school cricket field. At any other time it would have been a very funny story. I was too tense to laugh.

Even over a telephone, Neil was nobody's fool. After a moment or two he said, "Joanne, is something the matter? Are you ill or something?"

He sounded so near, as if he was a mile up the road, instead of hundreds of miles away. It was cruel. He kept on asking what was wrong. Finally I began to explain. I kept stopping and starting. Not wanting to mention Mrs Delaney, thinking about the row we'd had, feeling worse the more I thought of it. Before I knew what was happening, tears were trickling slowly down my cheeks.

Neil asked what I was going to do. I wailed that I didn't know, apart from waiting for Brian to come home.

He made lots of encouraging noises, and that made things worse. I was sliding into a full-scale panic, disintegrating like a book that's fallen into the bath.

He tried to get me to calm down. I couldn't. Finally he said they'd phone back in the morning. When he hung up, the silence in the room was deafening.

Friday was an awful day. When I woke, my head

felt as if it was stuffed with modelling clay. There was a heavy grey mist right over to the nearest trees. The ones by the river were invisible. I'd forgotten to take any milk out of the freezer so I made up one of those lemon drinks with paracetamol in them and took it back to bed.

Lunchtime. No sign of Brian. I finally got up, but when I looked inside the freezer there was nothing I wanted to eat. The heavy feeling in my head was getting worse. I had a shower, with the hopeful but crazy idea that the phone would ring as soon as I was dripping. It didn't.

I went back to my still life. It looked so two-dimensional I was disgusted with it. The mist had lifted but I was reluctant to leave the house, so I watched an ancient James Stewart film, reading some magazines at the same time, so that my brain was well and truly confused by the time the film finished. I still didn't feel hungry, but I peeled potatoes enough for two, again with the idea that that might bring him. It didn't work any more than the shower had.

# 12

# Campbells and confusion

The evening wore on and the Campbells didn't phone.
That hurt.

I could understand it. They wouldn't want to risk
more tears and hysterics. I didn't have the nerve to
phone them. I knew it was silly, but I couldn't.

When I'd first met Roddy and Neil, we'd been like
strangers trapped in a lift. They'd been wary of the
English girl with the short temper and bad manners,
and I'd been downright hostile. But soon I'd learned
to respect them. They had shown me what courage
meant, and it was their faith in God that had made me
want to believe. So, even though I could understand
why they'd retreated from my cries of anguish, it hurt.

I was at the kitchen table, my head on my arms,
when a distant noise drew me to the window. There
was a white shape in the distance, down at the bridge.
A truck. A big one, like a removal lorry. The driver
must have lost his way. Sure enough, after a minute
or two it moved on, the engine noise harsh across the
fields.

I stayed at the window, not looking at anything in
particular. Then I noticed something moving along
our road. The shapes puzzled me, then became rec-
ognizable as back packs. Two people. Ramblers, I

guessed. Out for an evening stroll.

Slowly, slowly, as if bubbles were popping in my head, I began to hope. Began to disbelieve but hope at the same time. Out through the kitchen, head down, not daring to look up yet. Across the gravel, past Mum's old car parked tight against the house wall. Through the bright beech hedge, on to the track, and all the time the bubbles in my head rising faster.

They saw me, shouted, and I was running to meet them like a mad thing.

I thudded into the front of Neil's sweatshirt and thumped him and then Roddy.

"You could have told me . . ." I shrieked.

". . . think she's glad to see us?"

". . . probably broken my ribs. What kind of . . . ?"

". . . could have phoned or something!"

And we were all talking at once and laughing, and nobody listening and me walking backwards all the time, dancing like a performing dog, so that I almost fell, and finally we were walking back to the house.

Moments later, inside the kitchen, it was suddenly all wrong. They looked like strangers. They'd both grown though I hadn't. Their voices were lower. I didn't like Neil's hair. He'd had it cut far too short. I kept on talking, because I was nervous, talking rubbish, prattling about the house and the workroom.

Roddy didn't look so different. I wondered why he was still wearing glasses.

"I thought you'd got contact lenses," I said.

"He dropped one into his developing fluid," Neil said before Roddy could answer.

"By accident," Roddy said mildly.

"We've had endless fun since he got them. Did I tell you he lost one playing cricket? It was just so funny. Everybody turned round, because it looked like a catch he couldn't miss, and there he was grovelling on the grass wailing, 'I've lost a lens, nobody move!' "

"Well, it was windy," Roddy said defensively.

Abruptly, Neil clutched at his throat and made moaning noises.

"What's wrong?" I said hurriedly.

"Dying of thirst," he croaked. "Help me, help me . . ."

Roddy groaned quietly and we exchanged smiles.

As I boiled the kettle, I mused that maybe they hadn't changed all that much. Neil still expected the female present to make the coffee. And, typically, he went off to explore the rest of the house and the garden, while Roddy stayed in the kitchen.

He unpacked his camera things, anxious to check that they'd survived the journey. Then we talked a bit about school, and how his parents were, and what the weather had been like on the island over the winter. Nice safe topics of conversation.

I took a packet of chocolate digestives out of the cupboard, and sliced them open.

"Is this enough? There's plenty in the freezer. Pizzas and stuff."

"Later maybe. Mum made an awful lot of sandwiches. I take it he's not back yet," he said after a slight pause.

"No," I said, wishing he hadn't mentioned Brian. Neil was just coming into the room. He caught what we were talking about, but neither he nor Roddy said any more.

"D'you think I should phone the police?" I said finally.

"We thought you might have already."

I pushed mugs of coffee over to them.

The silence became uncomfortable again.

"If it's easier, I'll do it. If you want," Neil began. He was watching me closely. Maybe he was waiting for another outbreak of hysteria.

I nodded. Now they were here, I wanted them to make all the decisions.

"Write down the car registration. And his office address. What's the local number?"

I wrote down all the things he thought the police might ask. He took his mug through to the sitting-room. We found the number in the directory and I left him dialling.

Back in the kitchen it occurred to me that Neil had his other side too, that he could shed the clown act and be serious. Like Peter in a way. Except that behind Peter's clowning there was hurt and bitterness instead of easy confidence. The police would take Neil seriously because he would sound as if he knew what he was doing.

Roddy was at the sink, unpacking the remains of their lunch and rinsing out flasks. His shirt-tail was hanging out at the back under his pullover, and he'd taken off his trainers. There was a definite aroma of sweaty socks.

In some strange way, that helped. It was exactly what I remembered them doing in their own house. Outside was for trudging through heath and heather in your boots. Inside was for being comfortable and easy in your socks.

"It's a dreich-looking object, an empty banana skin," he reflected, holding one up before dropping it into the bin.

"Roddy, I still don't understand how you got here so fast," I began, feeling the need to talk, not wanting to think what the police might be telling Neil . . .

"We came with the shrimp."

"You what?"

"Shrimp lorry," he explained. "They come down from the processing plant twice a week. He goes as far as Leeds. Remember Lachlan McLeod the postman?"

"Vaguely."

"His Uncle Donald drives one of the lorries. After we phoned you last night, Neil asked Lachlan and Lachlan fixed it with Donald. He picked us up at five this morning."

"And your mother let you?"

"She was worried about you. I think they'll come before Wednesday if we yell for reinforcements. As soon as Dad can get off. Mind you," he added, "if she'd seen the way Donald hammered down that road, she'd have had second thoughts."

Neil came back through.

"What did they say?" Roddy asked.

"Not a lot. They didn't have any report on him or the car. They'll phone back if there's anything."

"But they didn't mind? I mean they didn't think it was stupid to phone?" I wanted to know.

"Why should they mind? They get calls about missing persons all the time. The information goes on a computer. If the car's sitting anywhere, it'll be spotted reasonably soon. Right, I'm going to let Mum know we're here in one piece," he mumbled through a mouthful of biscuit. "You want a wee word with her?"

"I don't think so," I said, and that made me feel guilty too. Now that the first excitement of seeing them had passed, I felt as if I was living inside a dream. Going through the motions of talking, eating, drinking coffee, while my mind continued its own secret thoughts and fears.

"Where should we put our stuff?" Roddy asked.

"I'll show you."

The spare room was clean, but the beds weren't made up. Betty had been going to do that on Monday. Roddy helped me to get sheets and pillowcases from the cupboard on the landing.

"Hello."

"Did you ask me something?" I looked up.

"Twice, but never mind. I was thinking we probably forgot to pack towels."

"There are plenty here. Whatever you need."

"Listen," Roddy said gently, "stop worrying. He'll probably be back any time now. There's bound to be an explanation. If there's been an accident, we'll hear soon. Unless he's lost his memory. But, even then, he carries a wallet, right? People don't just vanish."

"They do. There was a thing on the news a week or two ago. They found a body in the back of a car in a lay-by."

"Don't be daft. Why would anybody do that to your father? Anyway, they wouldn't put it on the news if it happened more than once a year."

I shivered. There were goose bumps on my bare arms.

"There's a heater in the cupboard downstairs. I'd better get it for you. The radiators in this room haven't been on for ages."

"Joanne."

"What?" I turned at the door.

"Did we do the wrong thing?"

"What d'you mean?"

He pushed his glasses further up his nose.

"Coming down like this, without asking. We kind of assumed . . . Well, not that we felt we were going to solve everything . . ."

"No. I'm glad you came." I managed a smile.

"Good. So stop getting silly ideas, OK?

"OK."

He asked if he could have a bath, so I dug out some towels.

When I came downstairs, Neil wanted to go and look at the river.

"Put on a sweater and come with me," he said. "You're needing fresh air. You've a face on you like a soda scone."

He bounded upstairs to tell Roddy where we were going, in case the police phoned. I guessed he needed to walk off the frustrations of sitting in a shrimp lorry for hours.

The evening air was cool, but not cold. We went across the fields, stopping only when we reached the metal footbridge. Away to our left was Mr Wilson's farm. The village, a scattering of red and grey roofs amongst the trees, lay on the slope of the hill to the right.

Neil didn't think much of the hills.

"It's awful flat," was his first comment. "I don't mean it's not beautiful," he said quickly. "But it's flat." He leaned on the rail and studied the rippling water.

"What do you get here?"

"I don't know. Brian doesn't fish."

"What *does* he do?"

"Work mostly."

"Poor guy. What a waste. Buy him a rod for his next birthday." He glanced over at me. "How am I doing?"

"How are you doing what?"

"Forget it. Just this feeling I have that I'm talking to myself. You've uttered about eleven words since we left the house."

"I can't help it."

"Yes, you can," he said. "You know what you're doing? You're working yourself into a deep dark hole. I know you're worried about him, but you're making it harder for yourself."

"Am I?"

"Aren't you? I bet you've stopped talking to God, too."

"That's none of your business . . ."

"Oh, don't be silly." He straightened up, brushing flakes of rust off the knees of his cords. "Come on, we'll walk a bit more."

We walked without speaking as far as the first gate. The field beyond was full of young bullocks who looked at us with interest.

"Healthy-looking beasts," Neil said thoughtfully. "Let's leave them in peace." So we turned back the way we'd come.

"The devil's really got you in a dither, hasn't he?" was his next comment. It stopped me in my tracks, literally.

"What are you talking about?"

"He's been having a right good go at you. Making you panic instead of pray. And it *is* my business, whether you like it or not."

Anyone overhearing us as we walked back to the house would have thought we were mad. It was kind of strange. There we were walking along the side of a wheatfield, with birds twittering in the hedges beside us, while we talked about God and prayer.

But it didn't feel crazy at all. We talked about school after that, comparing notes about teachers who were sarcastic or made it hard for anyone who had a faith. As we talked, it suddenly occurred to me that even my best friends would never understand how you could go for a walk with a boy and talk about religion the whole time, and the boy not even try to hold your hand. And how they would say I was frigid or something.

Then I felt confused, because all at once I didn't know how I'd feel if Neil *had* wanted to hold my hand. And I wished I'd never thought about it, because I didn't think he would have anyway. I told myself he wasn't even good-looking, especially with his dark curls gone. He was practically scalped.

Back in the house, he said he was hungry. I found a tin of chicken in white sauce and began to make toast to go with it. Roddy heard us and came through to the kitchen.

"You missed the phone. Five minutes ago."

"The police?"

"No. Here, I wrote it down."

I glanced at the name, Larry Capaldi. It meant nothing.

"He thought I was your Dad. I said he wasn't here at the moment, was that all right?"

"Probably someone selling double glazing," Neil suggested.

Roddy scratched his ear. "I think he took me for someone else," he said thoughtfully. "Then maybe he decided the accent was wrong. He didn't sound happy. Do you have trouble with your neighbours or anything?"

I shook my head. A couple of seconds later I realized there was only one Larry we knew. The tin in my hands went out of focus.

". . . but I interrupted him, so he didn't really say much after that. Joanne, you're going to cut yourself."

Roddy took the tin-opener away from me, and finished the job. "There's not very much in this," he objected.

"There's toast too," I pulled out the grill pan and turned the slices just in time. "You said you weren't hungry."

"Well, I wasn't then, but I am now, and it's an awful wee tin."

I took another from the cupboard and gave it to him.

"That's more like it," Neil said. He seated himself on one of the chairs.

I got what salad stuff there was from the fridge and began chopping cucumber. What could Larry possibly want Brian for? They'd only met once. Or had they met somewhere else, yesterday? Had something happened between them?

Roddy must have been watching my face. He seemed to guess something was bothering me.

"Would he be a client of your Dad's, maybe?"

"No. And he *isn't* my Dad."

"Bang, bang, SPLAT," Neil said from the other side of the room.

I turned round.

"Article on punctures," he said innocently, holding up a car magazine he'd taken from the dresser.

"Here, you need a bigger saucepan." I handed it to Roddy rather urgently.

"It could have been a man who works for one of our neighbours," I told him, trying to sound casual. "I don't know if his name's Capaldi, but his first name's Larry. Brian doesn't like him. You'd better stir that," I added, meaning the chicken.

For a while Roddy dutifully moved the chicken pieces around in the pan, but Neil called him over to look at an article, and I was left with everything to do while the pair of them discussed it for the next five minutes.

"Well, are you hungry or aren't you?"

114

It sounded petulant. They looked at one another, then back at me.

They came over, sat down opposite me. I'd lifted my fork, then I realized that Neil was beginning to say grace. My guilty hand fell slowly back to the plate.

He didn't stop after the bit about the food.

". . . And Lord, we ask for Joanne, that you will help her right now, because you can see how things are . . . and may she know you are with her. Give her your peace, as you promised. And wherever Mr Barnes-Ingram is, please would you be with him, and look after him, and bring him safely home."

I thought I was going to be OK. But after a mouthful or two I couldn't see the plate. I kept chewing furiously, which of course didn't help. To make matters worse, I didn't have a handkerchief.

Dimly I was aware of Neil getting up. There was a tearing sound behind me, then a bundle of kitchen towel landed on my lap.

I blew my nose.

"Sorry," I said, feeling like a total fool.

"I'm making more toast," Neil announced. "Is there enough bread?"

"More in the freezer once that's finished," I said, sniffing.

He passed behind me, picking up the rest of the kitchen roll and giving my head a light pat with it as he went. I took a few deep breaths. I had to get hold of myself and stop over-reacting.

"I hope you don't mind," Roddy began, "but I had to use your soap. We forgot that too. I put the towels on . . ." He stopped abruptly.

"You haven't got a dog, have you?"

"A dog? No, Brian's allergic to them. They give him a rash . . ."

115

Neil turned from the grill, bread in hand. Roddy had risen from the table. He was looking past me through the French windows. I got up, but he stopped me, putting a hand on my shoulder.

"No, it's not important. Neil?" he said.

Neil put the bread down. He said something in Gaelic. Roddy answered briefly in the same tongue. Not understanding made me instantly agitated.

"What is it?" I said, swivelling round, but they ignored me. They'd slid the window open and were both out, into the garden, running towards the far bushes. I didn't know whether to follow or not. I shifted about on the patio slabs like a nervous canary.

Abruptly there was a yell, then several yells, and they were both on the ground, wrestling with something or someone!

# 13

# Name, rank and number

The scuffle was short. When I reached them, Neil had
the intruder up on his feet, holding him by the arm.

"Peter!" I yelled angrily. "What are *you* doing here?"
I could barely speak for fury.

"Do you know him?" Neil began, hesitantly. "He
said he's a friend of yours . . ."

"Let go of me, I told you . . ." Peter pulled his arm
away.

"You're an idiot, Peter. I've never met . . ."

I stopped. There was blood spattered on his shirt
and the side of his face . . .

"What've you done to him? You've hurt him!"

"*We* didn't hurt him," said Neil indignantly. "We
just *sat* on him for a moment or two."

"Maybe we should go into the house," Roddy suggested.

So we did.

Peter was a sorry sight, caked with dust and dried
earth all down his front. The white jeans would never
be white again. Blood had run from cuts on his arm
and the back of one hand. There was a large lump on
his forehead just at the hair-line. In the kitchen, he
slumped into the nearest chair.

"Oh, sit down, Neil, for pity's sake," I said, for he was standing in front of Peter, legs astride, like someone in an old war film. The first aid stuff should have been in the top drawer of the dresser and wasn't. I rummaged frantically. Why did we keep so much junk?

"I'm not moving till we get some explanations . . ."

"You're not helping, standing over him like the Gestapo."

Peter turned his head to me.

"Who are these creeps, anyway?"

"Friends from Scotland. That's Roddy, and the one playing at World War II is Neil," I said, slamming one drawer shut and yanking out another.

Roddy laughed from his chair, and said something briefly in Gaelic. Neil glowered at him.

"All right, your turn," he said to Peter. "Explain yourself."

"You'll get nothing from me but my name, rank and number."

"Funny guy, aren't you?"

"Peter lives in the village," I said hurriedly. "And he's bleeding, in case you hadn't noticed."

At last I found the box. I pushed open the lid.

"Hold on a minute, there's no point in cleaning his arm, with the rest of him in that state," Roddy objected. "He'd better have some of our clean things."

Neil bent forward and looked at the cuts.

"What did you do these on?" He almost touched the arm. Peter flinched away.

"Glass."

"In our garden?" I asked, puzzled.

"I broke out of the house through a window."

Now I'd heard everything.

"Peter, I don't believe you."

"So what were you playing, Superman?" Neil asked curtly.

"Neil," Roddy said quietly. Peter had straightened up. Neil looked right back at him. Then abruptly he said, "Oh, come on. We'll use the downstairs shower."

He picked up the box, and headed out of the room. Peter rose slowly.

"Coming to hold my hand?" he turned to me.

"You'll cope."

"If you say so."

He gave me a big smile, ignoring Roddy.

I took a bite of cold toast. Roddy took off his glasses, inspected them, then went over to the sink and began to clean them with washing-up liquid and a trickle of hot water. He tore a square of kitchen towel off the roll and dried them.

"All right," he said finally, "so tell me, who is he?"

"He lives in the village."

"Is this a village custom, jumping out of windows?"

I didn't know where to begin.

"Wait a minute."

I went quickly through to the sitting-room, found one of Brian's records and took it back to the kitchen. There was a photo of Peter's father on the back, in full evening dress, baton in hand. It was in colour and he looked very dynamic and handsome. Below it was a quote from *Gramophone* magazine: "Niemenen conducts with such finesse that the music flows of its own accord."

"That's his father," I handed it over.

"Carl Niemenen? Here?"

"Their house is on the far side of the village. Peter's OK," I added, "except he's a bit of an idiot."

"You mean he's simple-minded?"

I tried to explain what I knew of Peter Niemenen.

How you never knew where you were with him. I told Roddy how his mother had died, and about his sister being handicapped.

". . . but I think he handles her wrongly too. And he actually said he hates his father, but I don't think he does. He just gets his own way too much, I think."

Roddy read down the sleeve.

"Does he come here a lot? Is Brian a sort of substitute for his own father?" he said.

"Brian? You're kidding. Brian doesn't approve of him."

Our eyes met. He smiled briefly, almost as if he'd said something wrong. Suddenly I got it. He thought Peter was my boyfriend. My face went hot. How could I put him right? It wasn't anything like that.

"I don't know why he's here, any more than you do."

"I expect he'll tell us," Roddy said evenly.

I filled the kettle and switched it on. Why on earth *was* Peter here? It was his escaped jail-bird routine again, like the first time we'd met.

"Don't you want that heated?" I said, seeing Roddy hesitantly forking over the cold chicken mess.

"It's OK cold."

He looked at the record sleeve again. In the silence I could almost feel his mind leaping from one wrong conclusion to the next.

"I can't think why he came here," I said again, trying to sound casual. "I didn't think he knew where we lived."

"Oh well, it's good practice for Neil anyway."

"Why?"

"He's decided he wants to do medicine."

"But you have to be brainy to get into medical school."

I didn't realize how rude that remark sounded till it was too late. He grinned at my confusion.

"I agree. It doesn't show," he said with a laugh.

He picked up Brian's car magazine again and, while he read, his fingers felt for toast that wasn't there. I had to laugh. He looked up.

"Sorry, I finished it. There's chocolate cake."

"Toast would be better. Or crackers. To keep the calories under control."

I'd forgotten he was diabetic.

"D'you have to be careful all the time?"

"Fairly careful. Brian doesn't have any health problems, does he?"

I shook my head, unwilling to think about Brian.

"Suppose he felt ill?" Roddy suggested. "Like he was getting flu. If he felt rotten he could have decided to stay overnight somewhere."

"He told the people at the office he was working at home."

"When?"

"Yesterday morning. He phoned them."

"Could he have been back there today?"

"He'd have phoned *me*. Chloe knew I was upset. And, besides, he hasn't got his house keys. Look, I'm coping brilliantly when we don't talk about him, so let's not talk about him, OK?"

He made a solemn mime of zipping his mouth.

He was only trying to help. He didn't know what I was holding back — the dark and hateful possibility that Brian might be with Mrs Delaney. That idea was worming its way to the surface like a monster inching its way up from the slimy depths of a marsh.

The other two came back, Peter now neatly bandaged, in a different shirt and a pair of navy cords. He sat down carefully at the table, opposite Neil. The record still lay there. He pulled it by the corner till the photo of his father was the right way up.

"How are you feeling now?" I blurted out.

He stared fixedly at the image on the cover for a moment then looked at me. My smile felt as if it had been stuck on with tape. *He* wasn't smiling anywhere. His early bravado had evaporated. There was a tight, tense look in his eyes.

"Peter?"

"He says Tarzan isn't back yet," this with a nod at Neil.

The twins looked puzzled.

"It's an 'in'-joke," I said hurriedly. "He means Brian. There's something wrong, isn't there? Did you honestly jump through a window? Did that have anything to do with Larry phoning here?" I added, remembering.

He stiffened.

"He phoned *here*? What did he say?"

"Who is Larry?" Roddy asked, bewildered. Neil leaned forward, rubbing his hand over his cropped curls, as if the whole thing was making his head ache.

"Well, did it?" I repeated.

"I came out through the window, because he locked the door on me," he said wearily.

"Look," Neil broke in, "could somebody explain what this is all about?"

"Didn't he tell you," I began, "when you were doing the bandage?"

Neil muttered something darkly in Gaelic.

"No more Gaelic," I yelled, thumping the table. The three of them looked startled. "Peter, explain yourself before I begin screaming. And start with Larry."

He started with Larry. He talked to the table, stopping now and then, as if trying to clear his head. He told us how he'd disliked Larry from the beginning, when he'd come home at the end of term to find the previous chauffeur gone and Larry established in everyone's good books. How his father had refused to take him to America as planned, and how Larry snooped on his every move. He told us about finding the gun. I asked why he'd been in Larry's room. He said he'd been going to put itching powder in his bed. I groaned. He admitted with a shrug that it had been a "kid's trick".

Things had come to a head that afternoon. Mrs Burchfield and Karen had gone to the hospital where she was to stay for assessments.

"I was saddling up Tequila when Larry came into the stables and ordered me to my room."

"*He* ordered *you*?" I said incredulously, then wished I hadn't. It made him sound like a coward.

"Did he cut you?" Roddy asked quickly.

"That was the window. I broke it with a chair. He'd locked the door on me. I said . . . well, I said he'd be fired once Father knew about him. He said Father knew about him already, and there would be some-body along to sort me out, or something like that. I couldn't stand it, being locked in like that. I put a tape on loud, and broke the window. I came across the fields."

I thought of the phone call to America.

"Peter, would your father have got your message by now?"

"I don't know. He hasn't phoned me."

Neil wanted that explained, so Peter explained it. Unless you knew Peter, it sounded very sensible.

I didn't know what to think. Was there more he wasn't telling us? Had he given Larry good reason to lock him up? I could imagine Larry getting angry. But was he a criminal? I felt like a juggler's plate on top of a bendy cane, uncertain which side to come down on, spinning and spinning . . .

Peter wanted to know what Larry had said on the phone. Roddy told him all he could.

I was getting stretched too thin, like the lip of a bowl in pottery class. Self-preservation made me angry and sharp.

"What were you planning to do? Hide in our attic?"

"I thought your father would help."

"Did you? Well, he isn't here, is he?"

"How was I supposed to know? Where is he anyway? Still dining with the dark lady?"

Roddy began to say we'd phoned the police. I interrupted, my voice high, brittle as old wire.

"Where are the dirty clothes? In the shower?"

"Leave them just now, Jo," Neil began.

"You can't leave bloodstains," I snapped, "I'll put them in the machine."

Wonderful methodical Betty. In the tiny utility room everything was in its place. I found a bottle of liquid stain remover. The cap was stiff, so I ran it under the hot tap.

"Need any help?"

I glanced round and saw Peter.

"Go away."

The top gave at last. I spread his sweatshirt on the stainless-steel grooves beside the sink, wetting the stains with cold water. I poured drops of the clear liquid on to them. My hands were shaking. Peter came right into the room and leaned against the wall.

"If I put my foot in it back there, I apologize."

I picked up the brush and began to work the liquid in.

"I'm sorry."

"Me too. Go away."

"Listen, I'm apologizing. What does it take with you? Don't rub at it like that, you'll make a hole."

I flung the brush into the sink. It bounced out on to the floor. "You know everything, don't you, Peter?"

"Not everything. One or two things I know. Like you can't go through life with a bucket over your head . . ."

"Buckets? Is that what you used when you flew through the . . ."

". . . don't take it out on me, OK? I know you're . . . well, you've got pretty strong ideas. I'm not saying you're wrong. I am not criticizing your beliefs." He spread his fingers wide for emphasis. "But it's a big bad world out there, whether you like it or not."

"What point exactly are you trying to make, Peter?"

"The point that you can't change people. If Brian is that kind of guy, you are not going to change him. I didn't think you liked him that much anyway . . ."

My heart was thudding in the silence. Was he right? My feelings about Brian were all mixed up but, when I thought of Mum and how she might be hurt, something seemed to tear at my insides.

"I don't believe he's with her."

"So you don't believe it. Great. I'm proud of you. But even if he *is*, is that the end of the civilized world? You're letting it *get* to you, that's all I'm saying. Let them live their lives. It doesn't matter that much. You have to not care what they're like."

"Like *you* do?" I wanted to hurt him, the way he was hurting me, to bring him down. He was all talk.

"Like *you* do?" I repeated. "Like the way you don't care about *your* father?"

# 14
# Muddy colours

Peter's eyes widened, like a child's when a balloon bursts. Then he straightened up.

"Those two creeps," he nodded towards the main part of the house, "why are they here?"

I opened the washing-machine door, scrumpled up his shirt and jeans and shoved them in. There was no way I could win against him. I poured a capful of detergent in and set the machine. There was no chink in Peter's emotional armour. Like old stains, his selfishness and bitterness were dried in. Nothing could shift them. I watched the water trickle round the sides of the glass. The machine began its heaving. All of a sudden I felt incredibly tired.

"Well, what are they doing here?"

"They're old friends," I emphasized both words, "and they came to help. They're using the house next week when we go away. Mrs Campbell's an old friend of Mum's from college. I lived with them last year when . . ." There was a thudding noise in the corridor. Neil skidded to a halt in the doorway.

"Phone call. Come on. Roddy's got it."

I ran after him.

Roddy turned, hand over the receiver. "Mrs Denny or something," he said rapidly. "I told her your Dad's not here. She won't believe me."

I took the phone from him, my stomach cold. She insisted on speaking to Brian. Her voice was slurred, and I wondered if she was ill.

"I haven't seen him since Thursday, Mrs Delaney," I interrupted. "Have you?"

No, of course not, and she'd been at the jolly office at the time appointed and did I think she had jolly well nothing better to do . . .

"Well, we've been in touch with the police," I said.

She stopped in mid flow.

"What did you say? The police?"

"In case he's been in a crash or something."

"A crash? Where was the crash?"

"I said, in *case* there's been a crash."

I could hear her breathing at the other end, and faint music that sounded like Radio One, then abruptly she hung up.

She hadn't seen him. Her anger made me certain of it. I'd been worrying about nothing. Relief swept through me like a bright warm wave. Thank goodness I'd said nothing to the police about her. Thank goodness I hadn't tried to contact Mum. I'd probably have blurted out something to her about my suspicions.

I realized Roddy was talking to me.

"I was asking who it was."

"One of Brian's clients." From deep inside a smile formed and broke on my lips. "No one important," I added.

I still didn't know where Brian was, but at least I knew where he wasn't. Hope stuck its head up, like a spring crocus breaking through winter soil. I began to believe that the explanation would be simple. He must have had trouble with the car. He'd be back soon. All I had to do was wait. Everything would be fine.

They were both looking at me curiously.

"I'm going to sit outside," I announced. "Help yourselves if you're hungry."

I needed a breathing space. Let them cope with Peter for a while. Maybe if we all ignored him, he'd stop fooling about and go home.

It was around nine, or just after, and still warm. The house martins were darting about looking for food for their offspring, swooping under the telephone wires. Above the fields the sky was huge and serene. There was hardly any breeze, and the smell of the roses was heavy.

I'd picked up my one book on Renoir on the way out. I'd reached the part where his arthritis was getting worse. He was working away with the brush fixed rigid in his bandaged hand. I looked at my own, and tried to imagine what it would be like to be crippled. I thought of Karen with her callipers and wheelchair. If she was seriously interested in drawing, maybe Mum and I could do something to encourage her.

Later on, I heard the washing machine coming to a stop, so I got Peter's clothes and hung them on the line. Then I went back to the garden seat.

Was he really going to stay? If Brian came back and found Peter in residence he'd hit the roof.

Wait a minute, said a little voice in my head. Stop hiding. What if Peter is telling the truth? No, it was too much. Larry couldn't be a crook. Think about it, said the voice.

I had to force myself to think. It was like trying to paint with a messy palette; the colours were muddying one another.

Suppose Larry *had* locked him in. Why would he have phoned Brian, if he was up to no good? It didn't make sense. Larry gave me the shivers, but

Carl Niemenen would hardly employ a criminal.

And was there really a gun?

I recognized again how isolated our house was. Mr Wilson's farmhouse seemed disturbingly far away. The nearest sign of life was the traffic on the distant road. I watched a car turn at the top of the hill.

It disappeared behind the line of beeches then came in sight again. A smallish white car. Not Larry. I relaxed my grip on the bench. Their car was black. Not Brian's either, unfortunately.

Unless, I thought, unless he's had to hire one. I waited for it to stop just past the stone bridge, because anglers often parked there, but it didn't stop. It turned on to our road.

It had to be Brian. I flew into the house, to the downstairs shower-room, rubbed a wet sponge over my face and tried to tidy my hair a bit. Leaning over the washbasin, I prayed hurriedly, "Thank you that he's all right. Please, please, Lord, make things right between us. I'm sorry I was so rotten. And don't let him go crazy because Peter's here."

I stepped into the passageway. Peter almost knocked me down.

"Where are you going?"

"Outside. Call me back when they've gone."

"But you wanted to speak to him," I argued. "You said that was why . . ."

"I know what I said. Just call me when they've gone, OK?"

The twins were at the sitting-room window.

"What's the matter with Peter?" I asked.

I glanced out. Saw the tail-end of a police car.

The doorbell sounded. I stared at Neil. His dark eyes told me we were thinking the same thing. Bad news.

The bell rang again, and I couldn't move. Roddy went to the door. Feeling unreal, I followed.

A police sergeant in shirt-sleeves filled the doorway. His long thin nose looked as if it was trying to get in touch with his chin. Behind him was a policewoman, young and pretty.

Dimly I understood he wasn't saying that Brian was dead or hurt. They were following up our phone call. We backed into the kitchen.

Sergeant Nose took off his hat and laid it on the table, beside the mugs and dirty plates. He was mostly bald, except round the sides. Two black tufts still survived in isolation on his forehead.

He was so quietly spoken it was hard to catch his words. He took out a notebook. We talked about the car, and what Brian had been wearing. He asked if I'd had any further ideas about where he might be. I hadn't. The policewoman smiled gently all the time.

Once he'd finished with me, he turned to the twins.

"Not from the village, are you, boys?"

Roddy said no, they were on holiday.

"From Scotland? That's a long way. Lovely part of the world, mind you. My granny came from Berwick." He added thoughtfully, "Wonderful woman. Never wore a hat, even in the snow. Relations are you, or just friends of the family?"

He asked for their home address.

"Just to keep things right. My boss is a proper terror for paperwork. Am I right, Margaret, or am I not?"

The policewoman smiled.

"Just the two of you, are there?"

"Our parents are arriving on Tuesday."

"Ah, that's good. Still, I expect Mr Barnes-Ingram will be back before then. Well, we'd better get on. If anything else comes to mind, just get in touch."

We went to the back door. The edge of the sky was turning a watered-down sienna, thinned by the heat of the day.

"I hope they're not making you do all the work, Miss." He gestured at Peter's shirt and jeans hanging limply from the line.

"Oh, we're well trained, right, Jo?" Neil said quickly.

The patrol car bumped away down the track. Roddy went back into the house, but I caught Neil's arm.

"Why didn't we tell them about Peter?"

"Because he didn't want us to?" he suggested. He broke off a withered pink rose from the climber at the door. "I'd like to know too. As soon as we saw who was coming, he bolted." He tossed the rose head over on to the grass cuttings in the wheelbarrow.

"Jo." It was his turn to slow me down as I turned away.

"What?"

"D'you want me to be nice to him or don't you?"

"What are you talking about?"

He met my eyes, then looked away.

"This Larry he keeps going on about," he said next. "Have you met him?"

"Once or twice. He's horrible. What did you mean, be nice to him? Does it actually matter what I want?"

"He says he can't go back. He's sticking to his story, that Larry locked him in. You know him better than we do. What do you think?"

"Neil, I didn't ask him to come and I don't want him to stay."

"But if he's in trouble . . ."

"*I'm* in trouble," I stabbed at my breast-bone angrily. "That's why you came, remember?"

"Calm down."

131

He put a hand on my shoulder. I shook it off.

"I'll calm down when I feel like it! And, right now, I don't feel like it. I've had it up to *here*, if you want to know, with missing step-fathers and police and phone calls. As far as I'm concerned, Peter can go and jump in the river!"

# 15

# Three in the morning

I went straight upstairs and locked myself in the bathroom. A huge moth startled me, flattening itself against the window, trying vainly to batter its way to the light. I lowered the venetian blind, and the skittering noise stopped.

I filled the bath. On the window ledge there was a *Peanuts* cartoon book of Mum's. She'd found a whole stack of them when we moved, all with yellowed pages and priced 2/6d, but they were still funny. I lay down and flicked over the pages. They were playing baseball. In one cartoon, the boy called Linus was fielding, out in the weeds, where he couldn't see the game.

That's me, I thought. Out in the high grass. Not on the path any more, in my straw hat, chasing butterflies, but on my own, lost in the high grass. Linus said he didn't mind being there, if it helped the team. Who were my team? Mum and Brian?

The water grew cold. I had to dress again since I hadn't paused for pyjamas or dressing-gown in my hurry. I switched off the light, opening the slats. The moth still clung there, motionless behind the steamy glass. I rubbed a hole. It didn't move. But someone did outside, down in the dark garden. I widened the hole.

Neil and Peter. Neil was sitting astride the low stone

wall, the boundary between us and the wheatfield. Peter was leaning against it on his elbows, facing away from the house.

I watched in frustration for a while, wishing I could hear their conversation, then I gave up and went to my room.

They were so different, I couldn't think what they'd have to talk about. I felt a flicker of guilt. It looked as if Neil was being nice to him, nicer than I'd been. Then I felt angry again. It was *me* who had the problems, *me* they'd come to help. It wouldn't have bothered me so much to see Roddy out talking to him. Realizing that made me uncomfortable.

I brushed my hair, wishing for the millionth time it was some other colour. The steam had made it hang in heavy clumps. Mum had never let me have a perm, one of the few things we'd ever disagreed on.

We'd been a fairly good team before Brian. She might have come to church with me in time, if we'd been on our own. The timing had been all wrong. If I'd been eighteen, leaving for art college, that would have been perfect. Instead she'd presented me with a step-father I didn't need. He hadn't needed a daughter either. We weren't any kind of team. And I couldn't pretend we were.

Brian had used the word compromise. That wasn't me. Some people ate anything. I loved Chinese food, and I loathed curry. I loved Naples yellow, and daffodils and yellow pansies and gold chrysanthemums. I loathed Danish blue cheese. I couldn't help the way I was. How could I live in the same house as someone I didn't like, submerging my feelings in a kind of emotional lukewarm bath, like the one I'd just stepped out of? And since that was how I felt about him, why did

I feel tonight that I couldn't bear it if anything happened to him?

Because I *couldn't* bear it. The sudden certainty of that shook me. I stared at my face in the mirror, unable to understand. Good grief, was this the girl whose biggest problem had always been whether to dye her pale eyelashes or go on using mascara?

The pillow was cool against my face. Below me there was a burst of noise as someone switched on the television, then the sound was lowered.

"Lord, where are you?" I said aloud. "I'm out in the high grass, Lord, and I don't know why."

I lay for a while, then put the light on again. My little red book was on the floor. I hadn't looked at it for days.

"Dear friends, let us practise loving one another, for love comes from God."

"Love comes from God." Love I didn't have, and couldn't dredge up from anywhere inside me. Love comes from God. I hadn't ever asked God to give me love for Brian. Not once. So was it all my fault?

Neil had said the devil was making things worse. And he'd convinced me. But nothing would get better if I didn't let God do what he wanted to. So, if he wanted me to love Brian, he'd have to give me the love. I'd have to ask him for it.

By the time my praying was done, the pillow was wet. I turned it over. I was exhausted. I didn't know what I was going to do about anything. But, for the first time in days, I *knew* that God was still in control and that he would not let me go. The grass was high, but he was higher.

There was a bell ringing in my dream. Dimly I realized I was in bed, and the bell was real. Telephone.

Out to the landing, struggling into my dressing-gown. Everything was dim and unreal. It couldn't be morning. The phone in Mum and Brian's room was the nearest.

Recognizing Mrs Delaney's voice again, I felt sick. I said Brian wasn't at home. She told me I wasn't listening to her. She was right. There was a tap on the door. Roddy in brown pyjama trousers, hair standing up at the back, bare feet looking huge.

I held out the receiver.

"Me?" he said, puzzled, "Who is it?"

"That woman who phoned before."

"What will I say?"

"Tell her we've all left the country," I said wearily.

He took the receiver. I sat down, hugging the sheepskin rug round me. He began telling her very politely to go away, then his fingers stiffened on the curly telephone cord. He looked round the room.

"Pencil? A pen or something."

There was a ball-point in the drawer under the phone. No paper. He upturned a Kleenex box. I was so tired that I could barely keep my eyes open. The seconds stretched out. I looked at his feet. All toes and tendons. Feet were hard to draw. My imaginary pencil went round the outline of his big toe, along the instep . . . my eyes closed.

I jerked up.

"You're not awake are you?" Roddy said.

I forced my brain to concentrate. He'd hung up the phone.

"Did you get any of that?"

I shook my head.

Neil appeared in the doorway, in shorts and a white vest.

"Was it him?"

"Mrs Delaney. The one who phoned before."

"Oh, good grief," Neil yawned, ". . . hope you told her it was three in the morning."

"Going back to bed," I mumbled.

"Joanne."

Roddy was still holding the box of tissues.

" 's OK. You keep them," I said sleepily.

"What's up?" Neil asked.

Roddy replied in Gaelic. My brain shot into wakefulness as if cold water had been poured down my back.

I looked from one to the other.

"What's the matter?"

"She's a nut-case," Neil said shortly, "Making phone calls at this time of . . ."

"It's Brian, isn't it? What did she say?"

"We can't do anything about it before tomorrow," Roddy said, clearly wishing that he'd held his tongue. He and Neil were exchanging looks.

"Roddy, tell me," I repeated, my voice rising.

"You might as well," Neil told him.

"She said her husband knows something about Brian."

My stomach closed in on itself, cold as ice.

"Was that all she said?"

"Jo, the woman's neurotic, she has to be . . ."

"He runs a garage," Roddy squinted at the faint writing on the box, "West Prior Road. Know it?"

I nodded. One of the main roads going north out of the city. I'd been out that way with Mum a few times to a suppliers whose canvas was cheap.

"This is crazy," Neil cut in. "Rod, look at the time. Even if there's something to it, we'll handle it better at breakfast . . ."

I wanted to do something, run around in circles,

137

phone the police ... I muttered the last idea aloud, as I trailed out behind them to the darkened landing.

"Not now," Neil said firmly.

"Why not? They do night duty . . ."

"I don't. See you at breakfast." He made for the spare room. I looked at Roddy. He smiled in mingled encouragement and apology, raised his hand in a kind of wave and followed his brother.

I crawled back into bed feeling ill. If Mrs Delaney knew something, why did we have to wait? The police ought to know. Or was she sick? Her voice had sounded slurred, like the last time. Maybe she was drunk.

Out of nowhere came a longing for Mum, perhaps because I'd been in her room, where even the rug smelled faintly of her perfume. I needed her. I was a kid of five or six again and I needed her. I closed my eyes. I could feel her, stroking back the hair from my temples, as she'd done when I'd had measles, her long cool fingers smelling of lemon handcream. I cried myself to sleep.

# 16
# Decision time

I woke up, feeling uneasy. Then I remembered all the reasons why. In the mirror was a girl who looked as if she'd been in a fight and lost.

The bathroom was occupied. I scurried over to Mum's room, bolted the door, and used her wash-basin. As I washed my hair, I wondered why I was doing it. Who was I hoping to impress? Just because I feel miserable, I don't have to look a mess, I told myself.

Do you think they'll notice? said the voice inside my head. Will *he* notice? I didn't want to analyze that. In fact, I didn't want to analyze anything. Somebody else could make lots of wise decisions today.

No more emotional scenes. I was going to be very calm and very normal. And I was going to love every-body, even Peter. Be calm. Love everybody.

The kitchen was deserted. I saw Roddy out in the sunshine, toast in one hand and a mug in the other.

There were small phials and a syringe beside the sink. I picked one up, then put it down carefully. I'd never heard Roddy complain about his diabetes. Did he never ask why it had been him and not Neil? Hadn't he ever moaned at God?

He turned, saw me, and waved. Moments later he came in through the back door.

"Did you get back to sleep?"

"More or less. Where are the others?"

"Neil's up. I think Peter's still asleep."

The phone call. Why couldn't he mention it first? I wanted to, didn't want to. I switched the kettle on, filled a bowl with cornflakes, poured in milk.

"Roddy, does it never get you down?" I gestured towards the sink.

"Not much. Well, only now and then."

"Why? I mean, if it doesn't upset you to speak about it . . ."

"It doesn't upset me at all," he smiled. "I've been fairly lucky. It's been stable, so I haven't had to miss a lot of school. I might get worse when I'm older, but it's daft to worry about that now. There's a lot of research going on . . ."

"Is that why Neil wants to be a doctor?"

"Could be," he looked amused. "But I hope I'll never be that desperate."

"What will *you* do? For a living I mean."

"Freelance photography, I hope."

The kettle clicked off. I made myself a mug of coffee.

"Roddy, what's Peter going to do?"

"For a living?"

"No, today. I mean, he can't really stay here, can he?" I tried to sound calm and loving.

"We talked about that last night after you went up."

"And?"

"Neil got him to open up a wee bit. Peter's convinced this Larry is crooked. We think he's right. He won't go to the police. He says they won't believe him, because it's his word against Larry's, and because," he hesitated a little, "he got into trouble a couple of summers ago."

"Well, tell me."

"He took someone's car and crashed it. I know," he saw my expression, "but at least he told us. Which wasn't easy. I mean, it didn't make him look good, did it?"

The door opened. He stopped speaking, but it was Neil.

"Right, folks, prepare to be overwhelmed," Neil announced. "According to the label, I am now 'shiny, manageable and healthy-looking'." He made scratching movements above his head.

"I'm telling her about Peter."

"Oh. Right. In that case, I'll be shiny, manageable and silent."

He helped himself to a mug, spooned in some coffee, felt the kettle and poured in water. Then he leaned against the worktop, looking out of the back window.

"But if Larry is after him," I said, feeling confused, "he has to stay here. Doesn't he?" I looked at Neil's back. No response.

"Maybe if Brian had been here," Roddy replied, "or if Dad had come down with us. But he said Larry was bringing someone else in. Reinforcements."

"So what do we do?" I fought down the rising sense of panic.

"All we could think of was going to the hospital, where his sister is. The housekeeper's there. He seems to think she'll be on his side. And he'll get a better bandage on his arm. We'll go with him," he pushed his specs further up his nose, "and come straight back. Peter thinks there's a bus around half past ten."

"Is there? What day is this?" I'd lost my grip on the week.

141

"Saturday."

"You'd better take your stuff, Rod," Neil gestured to the sink.

"Once I've had more to eat."

"I think there's bacon left." I got up and opened the fridge. My brain wasn't working properly. Neither of them had mentioned the phone call. I didn't know whether to or not. I felt like an overweight seal trying to get out from underneath an ice floe.

"But Larry could see you any time you leave the house, and . . ."

"Of course he could," Neil interrupted, "but what else can we do? We were awake till after twelve, racking our tiny brains. Look, I'll do that," he took the packet of bacon from me. "You get his clothes," he nodded in the direction of the garden, "so I can get mine back before he bursts all the seams."

It was a beautiful day, if you were interested in weather. A cerulean blue sky and just the faintest ripple on the fields. I took Peter's jeans and shirt to the utility room, and set up the ironing board. I could smell bacon frying, but it didn't make me want any.

When I went back, Peter was at the table, still in borrowed clothes. I held out his own.

"They aren't clean, but they're cleaner," I said apologetically.

"Any more bread, Jo?" Neil interrupted.

"In the freezer, in the back pantry."

"I'll find it," he said.

Roddy wasn't there. When I saw the syringe wasn't by the sink, I guessed he'd gone to take his insulin in private.

Peter didn't look a lot better than the night before.

"How's your arm?" I asked.

"Not bad."

"You did get covers and things all right, last night? I'm sorry you were on the floor . . ."

It took him a while to answer.

"I couldn't stand being locked in." He watched my face. It was an explanation. I sensed it was a plea for understanding as well.

"Sure," I said inadequately.

"It seemed like a brilliant idea. Because I thought your step-father would be back." Then, with a glance towards the doorway, he added, "I thought for a minute there, you know, that he was mainlining or something."

"He's got diabetes."

"He told me. He's all right. Both of them are," he added casually. Then he concentrated on spreading marmalade. I didn't know what to say. Those few words had cost him a lot. Again I wished I'd had a tape of the night's conversation.

"Peter, couldn't you phone your father again?"

"I don't have the number. He's doing the big concert tonight in Washington. Climax of the tour. I'd never get through."

"What big concert?" I asked.

He explained it was all Slavonic music. The President would be there, and a visiting Russian delegation in their best black ties.

"Once I get to the hospital, I'll be fine. Mrs Burchfield's worked for us for years. She'll believe me."

I believed him myself now. He seemed to have gained control of himself in some way. But his new-found calm somehow only increased my nervousness.

Neil came back with a loaf. I started on the dishes, and in a moment or two Roddy appeared. They talked about buses, then Peter went to change into his own

143

clothes. I swirled at the greasy plates, my stomach tightening with every passing moment.

"Have you got money?" I said abruptly.

"Why? Are we paying for this?" Neil was on to his fourth slice of toast. "Is bacon extra?"

"For the bus. I haven't got any . . ."

"Mum gave us plenty," Roddy reassured me.

". . . and I don't want to stay here on my own."

They looked at one another.

"I don't want to be here if Larry comes. It'll be better if we all stay together. I'll leave a note, in case Brian comes back. Goodness knows what I'll put on it," I faltered, "but something, so he won't worry. And anyway, when we pass a police station, I want to go in and tell them what that woman said."

"You could phone," Neil objected. "And honestly, Jo, the woman was havering."

"I don't think she was sober . . ." Roddy began.

"I'm not staying here on my own. If I don't get out, I'm going to crack up."

I meant it. I couldn't stay in the house by myself again. Whatever happened next, I wanted to be surrounded by people.

# 17

# On the run

The bus driver was enjoying himself. He scratched his head.

"Never seen one of these," he said thoughtfully. He held Roddy's Scottish pound note up to the light. From the front seat an old man in a brown suit with a waistcoat and a watch chain said with a chuckle, "Monopoly money, William. Don't you have none of it."

The game might have gone on longer, but a woman behind us called impatiently, "Get on with it, Billy, I've more to do than stop here all day!"

Roddy and I fell on to the back seat alongside the other two, as the bus scrunched into gear and moved away. We'd gone across the fields to get to the village, and seen no one, but we were all fairly tense till we left the houses behind.

"What was all that about?" Neil asked.

"A Bank of Scotland pound note."

"Och, well," Neil did his exaggerated Highland accent, "you were forgetting we are south of the border now, Roderick. Surrounded by foreigners and Sassenachs we are, by Chove."

We passed the weed-fringed expanse of tarmac where a wartime aerodrome had once stood. Neil asked Peter about it and pretty soon the three of them were deep in conversation about Lancasters and Mosquitoes.

I was next to the window where the sun was streaming in. At first it was pleasant, then I began to bake. I felt exposed too, unable to shake off the feeling that somehow Larry might have seen us. But the only car I recognized was the white police car from the night before. It came out of a side road, followed us for a few miles, then turned off towards Kirkby Waterfoot.

In the city, the bus depot was grimy, noisy and swarming with people. Peter and Roddy went to check which bus we needed next. Neil and I joined a queue at the shop. He wanted a street map, and I'd said I was going to drop if I didn't get something to drink.

The ground was speckled with discarded tickets and torn sweet papers. A pigeon with a lame foot pecked here and there at minute bits of food. In front of us a mother told her whining child she'd had enough of him, crisps were all he was getting. We shuffled slowly forward.

"What d'you want?" Neil asked as we neared the counter.

"Lime juice. Anything as long as it's cold."

The doors were open, but the hall was airless. We breathed heat, diesel and cigarette smoke.

"Neil, last night, what did you and Peter talk about?"

"Hey, d'you think I could get mine like that?"

A boy in tight black-leather trousers and a black T-shirt went past. His dyed blond hair was rigid with gel at the front, cutting the air before him like a spear.

"I'd have to stop sleeping on my stomach. Maybe it wouldn't work."

"What were you talking to Peter about?"

"Peter? Lancaster Bombers," he said after a pause for recollection.

"Not in the bus. Last night."

"Oh, last night? Lots of things."

The girl behind the counter sang out, "Next, please." Neil bought a map, juice and some mints. We turned away. There was a place to sit nearby on red moulded plastic round a column covered in adverts.

The juice was painfully cold. It ran like a clear white line all the way to my stomach. Neil had opened the map and was searching for Friarscourt Street and the hospital.

"What sort of things did you talk about?"

He smiled as if my persistence amused him.

"What you mean is, did we talk about you?"

"I did *not* mean that, and you know it. I just wondered how you'd been able to win him over so quickly."

"Natural charm," he grinned.

"I should have guessed. Did he talk about his father?"

"A bit. And his grandfather too. He sounds interesting. Did you know he was from this place in Russia where they're trying to get independence? He got shot in the war, fighting in the resistance. He's still alive, but Peter's never seen him."

"He told me something about it," I said, frustrated. What *did* I want him to say? It annoyed me to think they might have been talking about me. But it annoyed me if they hadn't. What did I *want* for goodness' sake?

Before we'd left the house I'd gone to change into a dress, the one Brian had chosen. I needn't have bothered. Neil's only comment had been, "Oh, come on, or we'll miss the bus."

"Roddy actually knew where Karelia was," he went

on. "Of course he's been into reading newspapers ever since the *Aberdeen Press and Journal* used two of his photographs."

"So you're all big buddies today."

"Of course. Wasn't that what you wanted?"

I should have been pleased, but I couldn't control this crazy new game my emotions were playing. Like wanting Neil to dislike Peter, because that would prove something . . .

"He's got a lot of problems, but he's had a bad time. It's pretty rough having a father who's brilliant at something, when you're a non-starter. He's been round the world a few times with him but they . . ."

"I suppose that's why he acts as if no one else knows anything."

"Oh, come on."

"Well, he does."

He looked steadily at me for a moment or two. I hoped he couldn't read my mind.

"Listen, dumbo, he's like that because he thinks he's a failure. He thinks he's useless. If I'd been passed around like a piece of left luggage the way he . . ."

He broke off. I turned. Peter and Roddy were coming, fast, dodging round the folk in their way.

"Quick!" Peter yelled, over the echoing noises of the hall. A second's hesitation and we were running too, across the floor of the station, out through the other set of doors. We didn't stop. The waiting queues were blurs of colour.

On we hurtled, heedless of traffic, round corners, nearly tripping on a dog's outstretched lead, across more roads. A cyclist wobbled, and shouted angrily at our backs.

Practically on top of one another, we came to a panting halt round the next corner. Stone steps led up to the ramparts of the ancient wall that went round most of the city. On the other side lay a park, flower beds and young trees. Beyond that, the river.

"Right, up!" someone said.

Up we went. Neil pulled me as I half ran, half scrambled up to the top. On our left, out of sight, the traffic roared past thirty feet below. On the right, sloping away from the walls, lay quiet gardens belonging to one of the city colleges. The sedate buildings sat beyond, shadowed by huge elms.

There was a bench a few yards further along, where the parapet broadened. We collapsed on to it.

"Sorry," Roddy said weakly.

"No. Great fun," Neil was panting too.

I didn't have breath to speak. My hair slides were loose, so I couldn't see much except hair.

"What was it?" he added. "Rabid dog or something?"

"Larry . . . at the shop . . ."

That much I heard, then they were all talking at once.

"Should have described him to you . . ."

"You're kidding. How on earth could he . . ."

". . . saw him watching us, but I didn't think, and Peter was asking . . ."

". . . and then he shouted . . ."

". . . think we probably lost him . . ."

The invisible traffic growled relentlessly, a monster with a grudge. Somewhere a church bell struck the half hour. At my feet the pale limestone slabs of the walkway were weatherworn, smoothed and grooved by years of use, A ring-pull from a can and some flattened cigarette butts reminded me what century I was in.

The pounding in my chest slowed. I closed my eyes

against the sun's brightness. Pinpoints of red and gold danced in the dark. I saw a black-haired woman in a scarlet dress, swirling, waving at me. Mrs Delaney . . .

Next thing I knew, someone was saying my name.

I brushed my hair back and concentrated. It was Neil.

"What's the matter?"

"Come on, we have to move."

He held out a hand.

"They're going to the hospital and we're going home."

"But Larry . . . He'll see them."

"We lost him. They're going to get a taxi. Rod's got enough money."

"I don't want to go home."

"Come on."

I took my hand back.

"I'm not going home, Neil."

"That's what you think."

Against the sun, I couldn't see him properly.

"I'm serious, Neil. I want to go to Mr Delaney's garage."

I didn't want to go to a police station and tell them what she'd said. Now we'd got this far, I wanted to try myself. Almost as if something was drawing me there. Now we'd split up, there was no need to worry about Larry any more. I knew where to get a bus to West Prior Road from this part of the city.

I drew my purse out of my pocket.

"Here," I said shortly, "You'll need the key."

"It's not a key I need, it's a ball and chain. Or a strait-jacket."

Again I tried to give him the key. He ignored it.

"You're a thrawn little beggar, aren't you?"

I stared back at him. Down in the gardens, birds sounded their high notes above the traffic.

"Oh, come on then," he said shortly. "We'll find this garage and be done with it. And a fine waste of time it'll be."

# 18

# Too many questions

"What are you going to say to him?"

I couldn't answer Neil's question. Behind the plate-glass showroom window, a line of gleaming cars lay waiting to be bought. Expensive, foreign and powerful. Mr Delaney might have more things to do than be polite to strange teenagers.

We passed from the sunshine of the main street through an archway to a square of tarmac. Wooden sheds and brick buildings with dull red corrugated iron roofs hemmed it in on three sides. The air was heavy with diesel and paint.

There were three or four cars, a taxi with its engine bared to the sky, and two red-and-white recovery trucks bearing the words "BestCars, 24-hour Recovery. T.A. Delaney". A man in stained blue overalls was bent over the taxi engine. A younger man wheeling a tyre from one shed to another glanced at us without interest.

We went through a door marked "Reception and Enquiries".

The receptionist wore bright green eyeshadow, a gleaming smile and gold, dangly ear-rings. She adjusted the smile when she saw what age we were. She had tiny flecks of pink lipstick on her teeth, which spoiled the image a bit.

I smiled. I became terribly well-spoken, avoiding Neil's eye in case his reaction would put me off.

Would it be possible for us to see Mr Delaney? If he had a moment? No, he wasn't expecting us. But it *was* rather important. I gave my name, adding that Mrs Delaney had advised me to come. I was rather impressed with myself.

She raked us over again, her eyes curious beneath the lime-green lids. Neil had picked up a glossy brochure. In his white short-sleeved shirt, he looked fairly respectable. He *was* different somehow, from last year. It wasn't just that his voice had broken. Or was it me? Was it the way I was seeing him?

She went away. I unclenched my smile.

"Are you coming with me?"

He put the magazine down.

"If you want. We'd better be quick. Roddy can't get into the house without us, remember. I still think you're daft."

"What was that word you called me before?"

"Thrawn? It means stubborn. There are a few stronger words in the Gaelic as well, but I'm too well-bred to use them."

The door opened. The receptionist beckoned to us.

"Please come this way."

My chest went tight. It *was* daft. What on earth was I going to say to him? He'd think I was crazy . . .

We followed her tapping high heels along a short windowless corridor to another door, which she knocked on and opened.

"Thank you, Sybil. I'll be along to deal with that other matter in ten minutes."

Which told us exactly how long we were to get. I sat on the only chair, across the desk from him. Mr

Delaney didn't look up right away. We were meant to realize we were interrupting a busy day.

He was quite good-looking, but overweight, and his ears were very flat against his head, as if they'd been glued on. His thinning dark hair was parted at the back, combed forward to hide the bare skin. The sleeves of his pink, white-collared shirt were shortened with metallic silver bands. His fingers were pale, bristling with short black hairs. At last he laid his pen down.

"Sorry about that," he smiled benevolently. "What can I do for you?"

My stomach was churning. I forced myself to go slowly. I said I was trying to contact my step-father, and Mrs Delaney had suggested he might be able to help.

"Sorry, love, don't think I know him. Maura must have made a mistake. Sure he bought a car here? What make was it?"

My heart fell. Neil had been right. I was only making a fool of myself.

"Mind you, we get a lot of customers. I don't see them all."

"He didn't buy his car here."

"Oh? Fair enough."

Now he was really puzzled. Over to me.

"Actually, Mr Delaney," I swallowed, "he's handling your wife's divorce."

He stiffened, looked at me, then at his desk pad.

"This says Fletcher."

"He's my step-father."

He looked past me, to Neil at the window.

"You the rest of the family?"

"Just a friend," Neil replied. He moved closer to my chair, resting one hand on the back of it.

Mr Delaney chewed his lower lip. His mood had

changed somehow. As if little grey boxes in his brain were opening and closing, offering possibilities, inviting decisions.

"I'm sorry, love," he leant back in his chair. "I've not met your daddy, and frankly," he laughed shortly, "I don't much want to, do I? I let my own lawyer handle everything. Poor Maura. Tragic, really. Alcoholic." He shook his head sadly. "They tell me it's a disease. I tried to help her, but there you are."

He pulled a cigarette from a packet on the desk and lit it using an onyx desk lighter. The acrid smoke strangled what air was left in the room.

"Still, that's life," he spread his hairy fingers in a gesture of helplessness and resignation, and stood up.

Interview over. He was a busy man trying to make an honest penny, coping as best he could with the pain of an alcoholic wife and a broken marriage. That was life.

From the rear of his room we passed into a narrow corridor. There another door opened on to the yard. Just as Mr Delaney reached for the handle, it swung in from the outside. A bulky man in a pale double-breasted suit came in on a wave of cigar smoke.

The corridor was narrow, and there were too many of us. Finally Mr Delaney stepped back, and we edged past. The big man in the pale grey suit said, "Sorry, kids."

"I have never felt so stupid in all my life," I began, once we were on our own outside. "If you want to say, 'I told you so', go ahead. Let's get out of here before I smash something."

Neil was looking towards the sheds.

"What's the matter?"

"Nothing. Just an idea. Look, you wait at the front. I want a look in that shed."

"What for? You can't go wandering about . . ."

"I think they've all gone for lunch. Wait for me. I'll not be a minute. I'll say I was looking for a toilet, if anyone asks . . ."

He was off before I could stop him, walking fast, behind the first truck and into the nearest doorway. I hung on for a few minutes, but he didn't reappear. I began walking slowly back towards the archway and the main road.

"Hey, kid!"

It was the big man in the pale grey suit.

He came right up to me. He wasn't as old as I'd thought. Nearer twenty than thirty. He just dressed old.

"Tommy says you're looking for your daddy."

I'd had enough embarrassment. I mumbled yes, and looked beyond him, willing Neil to appear.

"Where's your fella?"

I said he was just coming.

"Well, maybe I can help," he smiled. The odour of cigars washed nearer. His fair hair was layered, long at the back, like a woman's. His eyelashes were so light they were invisible.

"See, Tommy's a busy man, but I've got time on my hands . . ."

"It's not important," I began.

". . . and I don't like to see a kid unhappy, do I? 'Cause I've got contacts, see, and maybe, just maybe, somebody's seen your dad around, so why don't we have a little talk . . ."

I should have moved. I should have run, but I was too slow. Before I knew it, he'd grabbed my arm and kicked open the door behind us. I cried out. His sweaty hand fell on my mouth like a moving, hot fungus. It happened so fast. I was so astonished I did

156

none of the right things, like biting, or kicking where it hurt.

He pushed me before him along the corridor, his immense bulk forcing me along. I resisted. He tightened my arm behind my back. His other hand pressed tighter so that it was all I could do to breathe. "Be a good girl," his voice urged me. "Take it easy."

We burst out into a narrow cobbled alleyway. There was an old van; white, rusty along the edges. With his elbow he leaned on the handle and opened one of the rear doors. Then he flung me in. I screamed, twice, scrabbling for the side of the door, for a way to get past. He slapped me across the face.

He told me to shut up. Except that he said it more crudely. Then there was a long shining knife in his hand. Did I want him to use it? It was up to me. I wouldn't look nice. But it was up to me. He took my chin in his fingers. I waited for my neck to pop from my shaking body.

"Be a good girl, darling," he said, "and I'll take you to daddy."

Then he dropped me. He slammed the door shut.

Dimly I was aware of another door opening, banging, then we were moving. There were no windows. No way of knowing where we were going. We cornered. I slid into the wall. I braced myself against the side, clutching at a metal ridge on the floor. Stay calm, I told myself. The thing to do is stay calm. How well I'm coping. My cheekbone feels as if it's broken and my left arm is practically out of its socket, but I'm quite calm really, I told myself. Then everything broke like a plate shattering, and I was sobbing hysterically.

I began to pray aloud, desperate incoherent prayers that God would save me, would get me out of this, that Neil would somehow be able to find me. What would he do? How long would it take before he decided that I hadn't just wandered up the road? Would he go back to Mr Delaney?

But would *he* tell Neil anything? Who was this horrible man and why was all this happening? My face was throbbing wildly where his horrible fingers had left their mark, but it was worse not knowing why, nor where I was going, nor what Brian had to do with all of it.

We stopped. I lost my grip and slid along the floor into the end wall. He cut the engine. I could hear my breathing.

When he opened the door, the daylight was dazzling. It glinted off the shining knife in his hand.

"Right then, darling," he said softly. "Remember what I said? No noise, no mess."

Awkwardly I stumbled out. He pressed a buzzer beside a big green-painted door. The sun was hot on my head, but I was shivering. Far across some waste ground, too far away, cars swished past on the dual-carriageway.

There was movement behind the door. Locks clicked.

The man who opened the door saw me and looked confused. He was big like the other man, but his face seemed unfinished.

"Who the 'ell's she?" he asked slowly.

"She's the jackpot, Frankie," was the answer. "We've just won the big one."

"What you mean, jackpot? I don't do them now, Snowie, you know I don't . . ."

"Forget it, son. How's our visitor?"

"He's OK, Snowie. I done everythin' you said."

I was walking between them, with the man called Snowie holding my arm again. My legs were shaking.

The place looked like a workshop, with shelves holding coils of wire and plastic tubing and tins of paint. We came to a door.

"You got the key?" Frankie had the key. He opened the door. I was shoved in so fast I nearly fell.

There was a man sitting on a sagging couch at the far wall. He looked up. His face was pale, his hair dishevelled. For a second or two, I stared at a stranger. Then, with the oddest sensation, recognition quickened in us both.

"Joanne?" he said, disbelieving. Stiffly, he stood up.

I went forward, stumbling, and then his arms were round me and I was crying into Brian's shirt, helplessly, hysterically, like a two-year-old.

# 19
# . . . and a few answers

"You look terrible," I said, trying to smooth the crumpled rag that had been a dry handkerchief minutes before.

"Thank you." He managed a half smile, drawing one hand over a stubble-covered chin.

"Brian, what's happening? Who are they?"

"I'm not entirely sure myself. No, keep it," he shook his head at the returning handkerchief.

"You're shaking," he added worriedly. "Are you cold?"

"I'll be all right. Honestly."

He made me put his suit jacket on. We were side by side on the lame sofa, at the high end, away from the broken leg. There wasn't much room to move. The place was packed with junk: empty boxes, paint tins, bundles of rags, even a couple of picture frames without glass. A moth-eaten Union Jack, half unrolled, lay on a shelf beside us. Daylight came from one opaque window, high in the side wall, covered on the outside with wire mesh.

"I know why I'm here," Brian began, "and what they want of me. But why me, in the first place, that I don't know."

"What do they want?"

"My signature on a statement." He brushed at his trouser knees. It didn't improve them. "Did they mess the house much?" he added.

"Whose house?"

"Ours."

"They haven't been in our house." In my mind's eye I saw the sitting-room that last night. I saw us arguing and me rushing out in a rage. I felt ashamed.

He turned me to face him.

"Let's take this slowly. If they haven't been to the house, how did you get here?"

"Well, I went with Neil to the garage, because Roddy and Peter decided it would be safer to go to Mrs Burchfield at the hospital, since Larry hadn't seen Neil anyway . . . What's the matter?"

He was looking at me as if I'd sprouted pansies out of the top of my head.

"Which Neil? And what garage, and who on earth is Mrs Burchfield?"

I took a deep breath and began to explain about Neil and Roddy coming. It wasn't easy, because I'm rotten at being logical. Our history teacher once said I had a mind like a delightful but trackless heath. Brian kept stopping me, saying things like, "When was that?" or "Why?"

But when I got to Mr Delaney's garage, and meeting Snowie there, he exclaimed, "Of course!"

"What did I say?" I asked.

"Tell you in a moment. Finish your tale first."

At that point there was a terrific rumbling above us, louder and louder till I thought the roof was coming in. I squealed.

"Only a train!" Brian yelled. Bits of dirt and flaking paint from the ceiling settled gently down on us. "We're under a viaduct," he explained as the noise died away. "Not the main line. There won't be another for a while. Go on."

So I did. I said Mum didn't know about him being gone. He said that was probably for the best, but I wondered if he meant it. He was very gentle with me. Even over Neil and Roddy coming he only said lightly, "Not sure if I approve of you spending the night with these two boys, Joanne."

Then I realized I'd left Peter out.

"Well, actually, it was three."

The parental jaw dropped. Hastily I explained about Peter and Larry. The gun, and the phone call, and how Peter had come like a refugee, dirty and bleeding, crawling through the fields, looking for Brian's help. I did *not* say that I hadn't believed him. I'd been wrong, but Brian didn't need to know that.

I watched his face for wrath or disbelief, but there was neither. Instead he said,

"Let's suppose for the present that the chauffeur is involved in some kind of conspiracy. I can't say I liked the look of him the other day myself. But, if your friend is correct in his suspicions, why me and not the police?"

"He got into trouble once for joy-riding. He smashed up a car, I think. When the sergeant came last night, he kept out of the way. Neil thought at the time he had a reason for it but . . ."

"Here we go again. Which sergeant?"

I realized that I hadn't explained that we'd reported him missing. As I said, a mind like a trackless heath.

"That's one comfort," he said. "So where is Master Niemenen now? With your friends?"

"Well, we got to the bus depot all right. At least we thought we had. Larry must have known somehow. He spotted Peter and Roddy, but we managed to get away. So he and Roddy . . ."

"Which he?"

"Peter."

"All right. I'm with you. Just."

"I keep forgetting what you don't know," I said weakly. "Anyway, Peter and Roddy have gone to the hospital where Karen, she's Peter's sister . . ."

"I do remember, keep going."

". . . is having three days of tests. Mrs Burchfield's there with her. It was the only thing we could think of."

"It didn't occur to you that Mrs Burchfield might be Larry's moll?"

"What's a moll?"

"Female companion. Bonnie and Clyde."

Mrs Burchfield with a machine gun? I couldn't see it.

"Not Mrs Burchfield. She's as old as Betty. And anyway, she's the secretary of the Women's Institute."

"Oh, in that case . . ." Brian nodded thoughtfully, lips pursed. "They'll be safe with her. Nothing safer than the old W.I."

There was a hint of a smile.

"Safer for you too," he added.

No more smile. This was the rebuke after all. I'd been waiting for it.

"But I . . . I wanted to find you."

"Yes."

"That yes is full of no," I countered.

"Could be." His eyes met mine. I couldn't read them.

"But it's a good thing I found you," I insisted. "I mean, Neil knows I wouldn't leave without him. He'll know something went wrong at the garage, and it won't be hard to find us because Mr Delaney must know that horrible knife man . . ."

"I expect so."

"So, even though he kidnapped me, it's a good thing really."

He was staring at his pin-striped trousers, but I couldn't guess what he was seeing. I'd been so glad to find him alive, and not in bits. And so glad our last horrible row seemed to be forgotten. Now fear began tickling up my spine like a tiny centipede.

"It isn't good, is it? Why isn't it?"

He straightened up, but he still didn't meet my eyes.

"It's hard to be sure. We're in the soup. Or in a pickle or a jam, whatever edible metaphor you like. It's hard to know if your arrival is going to get us out, or thicken the mixture."

"Well, I don't know anything," I protested, "Not even why you're here at all!"

"I'm sorry." He got up and stretched, as if his back was stiff, then he turned and leaned against the wall.

"I got to the office on Thursday, parked the car as usual. At the foot of the office stairs, I remembered a map I'd promised to lend George. It was still in the glove compartment. There were two men at the car — those two."

"What were they doing?"

"Opening the door. I yelled at them. Old Johnnie heard me. Out he came, at the double. He shouted too, once he saw something was wrong. I expected them to run from our righteous indignation. But they waited for us."

He picked a flake off an old paint tin, and flicked it into the air.

"And?"

"And naturally I asked what they thought they were up to. They were somewhat abusive. I told Johnnie to phone the police. Then the bald one gave him a vicious punch in the stomach. I tried to get to him. His heart's not good, I may have mentioned . . ."

"Yes."

"Our other friend had a knife against my stomach before I could do a thing."

He went on quickly. "Look, I told them, never mind the car, forget the car. Take it if you want. The old man needs a doctor, his heart's bad."

Brian's shoulders sagged, as if he'd lost a battle somewhere.

"It happened so fast. Later you try to think . . . was there anything that you could have done . . . anything? Despite the knife. You go over it, and you try to . . ."

"They took Mr Davis to hospital."

"How do you know?"

"Chloe told me. I phoned because you'd left your keys. He might be all right."

"I hope so."

I remembered Chloe saying how Brian cared about the old man, and I felt terrible. Now I realized that I'd only seen in Brian the things I wanted to see.

"They took the keys and made me drive. The one with the knife got in beside me. He made me phone the office, because I said they'd miss me. I said my wife was abroad. I lied about you," he said ruefully. "Told them I had no family. A couple of miles later we went off the road. I thought, here we go, into the undergrowth with the throat delicately slit, but instead they locked me into the boot, and brought me wherever we are now."

"I still don't understand . . ."

"I'm beginning to." He sat down beside me again. "You saw these characters at Delaney's garage?"

"Just the knife one."

"All right, then. Let's go back a little and take it slowly. I expect you know Delaney's wife is divorcing him. As a client she's a nuisance. Jackson took the case originally, but he was getting no other work done. Well, apart from anything else, Mrs Delaney has a drink problem. When she drinks, she talks. According to her, Mr Delaney has a profitable sideline finding cars for clients at special prices. I imagine he had a buyer who wanted a Mercedes like mine. With me so far?"

"Yes . . ." I said hesitantly.

"So, he knew what kind of car I drove and . . ."

"But he said he'd never met you."

"Then he must have a very selective memory. We *have* met. Mrs Delaney saw him with a woman in the Campagnola not so long ago, and began to make a scene. Delaney persuaded the manager to call me rather than the police. When I arrived, Delaney and his girlfriend were still there. It wasn't very pleasant," he made a face. "After they had gone, it took me about half an hour to calm her down, before I could put her in a taxi and send her home."

So that was what Peter had seen. Well, at least one part of the puzzle was cleared up. I tried to get the rest of it straight in my mind.

"So what you're saying is, he saw your car that day and then, when someone was looking for a Mercedes like yours, he sent those two men to get it?"

"That's my guess."

"Mrs Delaney said her husband knew where you were."

"Really?" Brian's eyebrows rose. "Did she say that exactly?"

"Roddy spoke to her." I frowned, trying to remember. "No. It wasn't *where*. I think she said her husband

166

knew *something* about you. I suppose she could have meant just that he was interested in your car. But Brian, he must be stupid to think he could steal *your* car and get away with it."

"But I didn't know those two were his suppliers. Without you, I still wouldn't know. Besides which, Mr Delaney might not know the extent of his wife's tale-telling. If Maura hadn't unburdened her conscience to me, I would have no reason at all to connect him with anything criminal. Nor can we assume that he knows we are here. Our knife-boy Snowie might be keeping that to himself."

I could feel my brain flaking like the paintwork. I didn't know how Brian's mind could go on working things out when he looked so exhausted.

"But in any case," he went on, "men like our Mr Delaney don't think logically. It would give him a disproportionate amount of pleasure to get back at me in that way. Our friends outside are the same. Anything is justified if it suits their immediate purpose."

"You mean they're stupid?"

"Oh no, not stupid. Irrational. In their own way, they're clever enough. Not Frankie," he added, "but the blond one, Snowie — he's smart enough for two. My one hope is that he's a little less clever than he thinks he is."

I didn't feel clever at all.

"You said something about a statement."

"He's written out a note to the effect that Old Johnnie dropped down of his own accord. In case he dies. I'm refusing to sign it."

"But you could deny it. Afterwards."

"Of course. And who would the police believe?"

"You," I said indignantly.

"Full marks. Of course, I would have to be around to deny it."

His meaning sunk in. He would sign it, and never be seen again. And me too. I felt a little sick.

Brian put his arm round me again.

"Don't worry. I don't think they're killers. Old Johnnie's collapse threw them into a panic, you see. I suspect they still don't really have any clear idea of what they're going to do with me. The statement is all they've been able to come up with. On the other hand," he rubbed his unshaven chin, "I wouldn't like to push them too close to the edge. And now that you're here, they might decide . . ."

He fell silent.

"Decide what?"

His lips were a tight line.

"What might they decide?" I insisted.

He stayed silent. But I knew. His fingers, clasping my shoulder through the jacket he'd lent me, they betrayed him and silently passed on the message. Snowie had said it at the door. I was the jackpot.

# 20
# Nowhere to go

It would have been easier if Brian had been angry. He was being so nice to me, I couldn't bear it. I kept my head down, but he saw I was crying again.

He took my hand and held it, without saying anything. But I had to talk. I only meant to say sorry for making things worse, but then I couldn't stop. It all poured out. How I'd been mad at Mum for getting married, and how horrible I'd been all year.

"But I know it now," I said tearfully, "It's as if I've been squashing it all down, all the things I felt, like squeezing a suitcase shut. But they don't stay squashed. Maybe for a while but not for long. And all those things I said. I shouldn't have said them. I wish I'd never said them."

"Maybe I should apologize too," he said slowly.

"Oh, no, it's me. I'm awful. I didn't even want to try . . ."

He had to see how awful I'd been. The last thing I wanted was for him to apologize.

"I said things I regret too," he insisted gently. "I could have tried harder. I'm lazy in some ways, you see. With your mother . . . she's so . . . Well, you see, I never had to work at loving her. It was easy, from the first day I met her," his face brightened for a moment, then grew serious. "But I have been at fault. I could have made more time for us to get to know one another. There was always so much work. But I should have passed it on to someone else, and got to know you. Because you are a person, aren't you, apart from being a step-daughter?"

"A horrible one."

"Now *you're* being irrational too. I don't mind you making my handkerchief sodden, but I won't permit irrational behaviour. That's the opposition's mentality, so behave yourself."

He was smiling. I tried to smile back.

"If you want to know the truth, I think you're the nicest teenager I know."

"You hardly know any." I blew my nose again.

"Oh, at least four. And I do owe you an apology," he added. His voice got quieter. "Part of the trouble was, you see, that you were the opposite of what I expected."

"How was I?"

"When Anne and I came back from Rome, I was ready for a rebel, someone fighting against all the adult values. Instead, you made me feel . . . How can I put it? You had everything solved. Including having God in your pocket."

"It's not like that . . ." I began.

"I know it isn't. But if you . . . Well, what I'm trying to say is, there I was at forty, still trying to work things out, and there you were at fourteen, with a faith like a rock."

"But I hardly said anything. I only talked about it once with Mum . . ."

"Maybe if we *had* talked more, it would have been easier. But I never gave you much of a chance, did I?"

I bit my lip, and my eyes filled again.

There was a rumbling in the distance, then another train thundered overhead. Everything was noise and vibration till it passed. Brian looked at his watch.

"I hope you like curry."

"Not much."

"I used to," he said ruefully, "but it's been curry, the whole curry and nothing but the curry for every meal. I fully expect Frankie to present me with a bill from the local takeaway before we leave."

After that neither of us spoke. I tried to understand what he'd said. It was strange, trying to see with his eyes. I knew my faith hadn't been like a rock at all. I'd been more like a jelly. Or a pathetic stuffed toy, sagging deeper into myself with every new problem, wallowing in self-pity.

Brian stood up again, stretching his arms and back. My thoughts went abruptly to Mum, wondering what she was doing. The Campbells might know how to reach her, so she might know by now that something was wrong. Then I wondered if Roddy and Peter had got to the hospital safely. I'd been horrible to Peter, in my thoughts, even if I'd been nice to his face.

Neil had been right about him. I saw that too now. It had always been easy for me to feel good about myself. I was only average at French and Maths, and Science had abandoned me as a hopeless case, but I'd always been streets ahead in Art. Maybe if I'd been a failure at Art, I'd have been as bitter towards Mum as Peter was towards his father. The thought frightened me.

I thought a lot about Neil. I tried to imagine what he'd have done when I vanished. Well, first, I told myself, he'll have prayed, which you haven't yet.

I leaned back against the wall and closed my eyes. I'd hardly begun when a comforting Bible verse came to me out of nowhere. I didn't even know I knew it.

171

"The eyes of the Lord are upon his children, and he rescues them from all their troubles."

I swallowed hard.

"Lord, I know you can see me," I prayed silently, "and I know you're here too. But we need the rescuing bit. And I don't know how you're going to do it."

Something very unheavenly had been bothering me for a while.

"Brian," I began hesitantly, "is there a toilet in this place?"

There was. "Revolting," he called it. Frankie let him go in when he'd eaten.

"How . . . um . . . bad are things?' he said tactfully.

"Not great."

He scratched his chin.

"Maybe we could manage something. He can't watch both of us. And there's a biggish window in the loo . . . He'll let you shut the door. You could be coy and well-bred. But if the window was stiff, you'd need to smash the glass . . ."

"I could try . . ."

"But you might get hurt, and how far would you get before he caught up with you?"

We never got the chance to find out. The door was flung open.

"Out," said Frankie's thick stupid voice.

I was behind Brian. He made as if to protect me.

"If you so much as lay a finger on her, you'll . . ."

Frankie told Brian to shut up or he'd expletive do it for him.

"Move it, both of you," his voice rose, "Snowie don't like waiting. And don't try nothing."

Snowie was waiting for us in the workshop. He took charge of me, letting us see the knife again, and reminding Brian how pretty I was.

Frankie opened the door, and we stepped out into a cooler, noisier world. They hustled us past doors and bricked-up arches, then under the viaduct, our footsteps echoing. In the distance stood a row of ordinary-looking houses, a corner shop with children on bikes at its door, a peeling bill-board advertising vodka.

A red car was parked half across the pavement. They made Brian get in the front, with Frankie driving. I sat in the back with Snowie. He put his arm round my neck. His other hand held the knife against my ribs. I felt its bright sharpness through my dress.

Brian asked where we were going. Snowie said wait and see. I remembered what Brian had said about them being irrational and I thought, they're going to kill us.

The radio had come on with the engine. The disc jockey was telling corny jokes. Soon we were driving swiftly through the back streets with an ancient Rolling Stones song in our ears.

Cars passed us unconcerned. My world had narrowed to nothing. I was a little person inside my own brain, shrunken and helpless. And the pressure that had begun earlier was now becoming unbearable.

"Please," I squeaked. My voice came out like an old woman's.

"You not comfortable, darlin'?" My companion stroked my hair. "I need the toilet," I said desperately.

His reaction was unprintable.

"I'm going to have to," I repeated. And truly, at that point I was more terrified of disgracing myself than of being hurt by him.

He took his embracing arm away, and shouted new directions to Frankie. There was a service station on the bypass. He told me to expletive wait, eyeing me uneasily. I'd become a child, instead of a hostage. He couldn't trust me to control myself.

Brian began to speak. Snowie yelled at him to shut up.

Our new route took us towards the city centre. We stopped with a jerk at a set of traffic lights. Snowie and I were thrown forward. Snowie cursed Frankie, who defended himself. The music pounded on meaninglessly.

The green light came on. Frankie was already in gear. At the next intersection he had to slow down. The road was narrowed by parked cars, and there was something happening ahead of us.

"Turn round," Snowie urged, and Frankie began to change gear, looking backwards. But there was nowhere to go. There was a car behind us, and one behind that.

I leaned to my right to try to see what was ahead. Snowie swiftly had his arm back round my neck, telling me to relax.

There were people, lots of people. There was a cyclist nearby, edging his way forward. A woman with a child in a pushchair crossed in front of us, so close I could see the metallic gleam of her ear-rings. Frankie revved the engine in frustration. My back hurt. My bladder was sending panic messages. This is so stupid, I thought. This can't be happening to me. Here I am, a knife in my ribs and a murderer driving me who knows where, and now we have a traffic jam and pretty soon I am going to disgrace myself.

We edged forward, following the brake lights of the car in front. Then a little faster. We stopped again. There were people all over the road, with banners, and placards on sticks. Frankie switched off the radio. We heard chanting, rhythmic clapping and laughter.

Frankie asked what Snowie was going to do about it. Snowie told him to shut up.

I moved with some vague idea of touching the window or the door. His hand tightened on my hair. I squealed. "Don't," was all he said.

I stared through the gap between the front seats, terrified now even to move.

And saw Larry.

And he saw me.

I closed my eyes. Opened them again, expecting him to have dissolved into someone who looked like him.

He was standing on the pavement. He took off his sun-glasses and held my eyes for a long moment, almost as if he wanted me to be sure it was him. Then he turned his back. I looked at Brian's face in the mirror. There was no sign that he had noticed. A few seconds more and Larry had disappeared into the crowd.

There were policemen now, directing the demonstrators to a side street. A huge poster, "Remember Hiroshima", dipped and swirled towards a shop awning.

There was a man in a dark-grey suit coming along the line of cars. He had a word with one driver and smiled. He came to Frankie's window, and gestured to him to open it. Frankie signed rudely back.

Then the man yanked at the door. In the same split second I felt a rush of air as the left rear door opened, and then it was a mad confusion. Snowie's hand tightened on my hair. I screamed. He was being pulled out, but he was pulling my hair out by the roots. Then Brian lunged between the seats, chopping at Snowie's arm. The pain in my head stopped, and I was on the floor of the car, but I was bleeding from somewhere because there was blood on my dress and the plastic of the seats, and my hands were sticky.

Someone grasped my shoulder. A man's voice was saying, "It's all right. It's all over." I could hardly hear him. Someone was crying in a high hysterical moan. The voice went on. Then I realized the moaning was me.

# 21

# Back from the edge

"There, that wasn't too bad, was it?" The nurse laid the empty syringe in a small metal dish.

She helped me turn over. I lowered myself very carefully on to the spot where the tetanus and penicillin shot had just gone. She raised the end of the bed and shook up the two thin pillows. I stared again at the line of stitches which decorated the upper part of my left leg.

"Very neat," she said approvingly. "Now, don't you dare move until Doctor comes back."

She lifted the cover over me from the end of the bed. "You can have your visitors now," she announced briskly, "but you lie quietly. No nonsense."

"When am I getting out?"

"Quite soon, I expect, if you behave yourself. Doctor wants to check your blood pressure in an hour. You went a bit faint on us, remember?"

She went out. A few moments later the door opened and Brian came through. He wasn't alone.

"Oh. Hello," I said awkwardly. I still didn't know how to speak to Larry, even though I now knew he was some kind of policeman. I'd grasped that much before the world had gone fuzzy at the hospital door, but there was a lot I still didn't understand.

"I've spoken to the sister," Brian began, sitting gingerly on the end of the bed. "She doesn't think they'll want to keep you in overnight. Is it painful?"

"I've got to take something when the anaesthetic wears off. It'll be really sore then."

"Apart from that, how are you?" Larry asked.

In sports jacket, white shirt and tie, he was so unlike his former self. That had thrown me when he'd appeared on the pavement. It still did. The early evening sun was shining into the room at an angle, into my eyes. He drew one beige curtain across the window.

"They said you fainted."

"I'm fine, honestly," I said defensively, "except I'll probably die if I don't get something to eat soon."

They both laughed. Then Larry commented, "Not much of a visitor, am I? After what you've been through today, I should have ordered something from Charbonnel et Walker."

"Who?"

"They make expensive chocolates," Brian explained with a smile. Someone must have lent him a razor, and he'd washed his face, but his eyes looked tired.

"They must pay you boys well," he added, to Larry.

"Not that well. Although I didn't think I was going to earn my money at all on this one. It looked rather a soft option."

"You're not a proper policeman, are you?" I said hesitantly.

Larry rubbed his nose. It was a distinguished-looking nose. Without the dark glasses, his eyes were brown and warm, droopy at the outside edges, like a spaniel.

"Joanne, we mustn't press Mr Capaldi for explanations . . ."

"No, you're due some. I was trying to think of the simplest way to begin. If there is one."

He pulled a grey plastic chair over, and sat astride, his arms on the back.

"I expect you both know that Carl Niemenen is in the States. Well, one rather important concert is scheduled for Washington. Tonight, as a matter of fact. He's conducting a programme of Tchaikovsky and Rachmaninov in the presence of the President. It's in honour of a Russian delegation who are over to prepare the ground for the next Summit Meeting. All right so far?"

We both nodded.

"Well, a few weeks ago, while he was still in Britain, someone sent Carl Niemenen a letter. In it was a prepared statement, which he was to read at the Washington concert. He was warned that if he didn't agree to do this, he and his family would suffer."

"Surely famous people often get that kind of mail," Brian said.

"True," Larry conceded, "but, in this instance, Mr Niemenen was inclined to take it seriously. You probably won't have noticed, but the Soviet authorities are having a minor crisis in one of their satellite republics . . ."

"Karelia," I declared confidently.

Larry and Brian looked at me in surprise.

"It was on TV and in the newspaper the day we went to Chiddlebury. Peter told us his father was born there. And that his grandfather stayed on after the war. Was the letter something to do with him?"

"Indirectly. Carl Niemenen's father is an old man now, but he was something of a hero during the war, and he still holds considerable power in the local party. It would be very embarrassing for the

179

Soviets if his famous son were to make a statement on behalf of those pressing for greater freedom from Moscow. That's what the statement was about, you see. It was a condemnation of the Moscow government and a demand for independence."

"But who sent it?" I asked.

"There's a sizeable community of Karelian exiles in the States," Larry explained, "including a few extremists. Since the letter came from America, we assume it was sent by them. At any rate, Carl Niemenen decided his son would be safer at home. He took the letter to the police initially, but because of the political overtones it became a matter for us."

"By 'us', I take it you mean Special Branch?" Brian said quietly.

"That's right. I was brought in to protect Peter and his sister. Mr Niemenen is being looked after by our American colleagues until he comes back. Then he'll be our responsibility."

"For how long?" Brian asked.

Larry shook his head. "That I don't know. Possibly until the Karelian situation quietens down. Or until we find those responsible for the letter. It won't be my decision. My own guess, for what it's worth," he added, "is that they won't, in fact, use violence. I can't see that it would do their cause anything but harm. Still, we can't be sure."

"So he's not reading out this statement tonight?"

"No. He's made that very clear."

"But he's going ahead with the concert?" Brian persisted.

Larry nodded.

"In that case," Brian said thoughtfully, "we should be applauding the man's courage."

"But why couldn't he have told Peter?" I objected.

Larry looked uncomfortable. He rubbed his nose again.

"On balance," he said at last, "it would probably have been the wiser decision. I've a feeling my boss will tell him that when he sees him. He may have already, over the wires. Mrs Burchfield knew what was happening of course. And the little girl's yearly assessments were rearranged so that she would be here over the crucial few days. A private 'nurse' will go home with her next week for added protection.

"To be perfectly frank," he went on, "I wasn't at all comfortable as a chauffeur. But my hands were tied. And you see," he slowly stroked his beard, "to be fair, Peter's track record suggested he'd resent being protected. He's hardly . . . well, I suppose it boils down to the fact that his father didn't trust him to behave."

"Then he needs his head examined," I muttered angrily.

"Joanne, please," Brian protested.

"Well, it's true. He should have trusted him. He should have talked it over. Except he was too busy, I suppose. It's not Peter that's the failure, it's him, if he doesn't try to understand how Peter feels. Maybe he doesn't even want to . . ." I faltered. I was getting into deep water. Brian was watching me, and I knew why. Understanding hadn't been *our* strong point either.

"I mean, we thought you were in the Mafia," I said quickly, looking back at Larry, "when we found your gun . . ."

"That was unfortunate," Larry admitted, with a rueful nod. "I've already had my knuckles rapped. I shouldn't have left it lying around. Young Peter phoned New York," he told Brian, "and naturally, Niemenen senior made waves. I was told to keep Peter at home till my boss arrived. He was to put him in the picture and convince him of the need to be sensible. I wasn't succeeding on my own. In fact, I'm not exactly coming out of this covered in glory."

"I imagine you saved our lives," Brian said quietly.

"Possibly."

"If you like, I shall stress the point quite forcibly with your superiors."

"Thank you. On the other hand, when I decided to leave the four of them together last night, it didn't occur to me that . . ."

"Did you know Peter was with us?" I asked incredulously.

"Of course."

"But how?"

"I guessed he would come to you. For money, if nothing else. I telephoned, but of course you weren't there," he turned to Brian again.

"And if I had been?"

"I'd have put you in the picture and come over. When I checked up on you, I found you'd been reported missing. That worried me, although it wasn't my particular headache. I'd established your good character by then."

"Thank you," Brian said mildly.

"It seemed a reasonable idea to have the local boys go over and take a look. Naturally, we'd kept them informed from the start."

"But they didn't see Peter," I objected.

"They saw Peter's clothes. Joanne had washed them," he smiled across the bed at Brian, "and hung them out to dry. Sergeant Woolsey reported that you were all nice and cosy. We decided to leave you till the morning, when my boss was due."

"You knew we'd taken the bus?"

Larry nodded.

"Did we really lose you, when we ran out of the bus station?"

"Temporarily. Fortunately, by the time I cornered Peter and your friend, I had two police constables with me."

The door opened. The nurse looked round it.

"I said ten minutes and you've had fifteen," she said sternly. "We want a nice normal blood pressure when Doctor comes back."

"We'll need a statement," Larry said apologetically. He rose from the chair and replaced it by the wall. "But not till you're feeling better."

"Out, please," the nurse held the door, and tried to look fierce.

"Apart from the cut, I'm fine, honestly."

"I'm very glad to hear it. But take it easy, anyway."

With that he went out. The nurse followed him.

"I'm going to phone Anne," Brian said. "Can I tell her truthfully that you're all right? Even at that distance, she'll know if I'm hiding . . ."

"Can't I speak to her?" I interrupted urgently.

"Hey, calm down," Brian said anxiously. "This is just going to be a brief call. Tonight when I've got you safely home, you can talk to her for an hour if you like." He smiled. "My guess is that she'll want to get the first available flight home, but it would be better if she wasn't worried sick as well."

I lay back on the pillow. He was probably right. If I only had a few minutes on a hospital phone, I might sound so desperate for her that I'd only upset her.

"I'm OK. Honestly. I'm sorry about the dress, though," I added. They'd put me in a hospital paper gown. My beautiful dress, spattered with red, lay in a plastic bag on a side table.

Brian smiled. "I imagine Betty will look on it as a challenge."

"She will, won't she?" I agreed.

"I'll be right outside," he added reassuringly, "if there's anything you need."

"Food," I said pathetically.

"Can't you wait till we get home? No, I see not," he smiled broadly. "Right, I'll do my best. Oh, by the way," he turned at the door. "Old Johnnie's all right. Still in intensive care, but they think he'll pull through. I think we might be back on the road," he added thoughtfully.

I smiled back. He didn't just mean Mr Davis. He meant us. Back on the road. Back from the edge. He felt it too. Thank you God, I said silently.

When he'd gone, it wasn't long before I began feeling frustrated. I wanted to get out. Thanks to that bossy nurse, I'd not been able to ask half the questions I wanted to. Such as how Larry had managed to be in the right place at the right time, and what Neil had done, and where they all were right now.

I stood by what I'd said about Peter's father though. I hoped someone would tell him he'd been a stupid idiot. It was time he stopped jetting round the world and . . .

Then I realized I was still doing it. Still brilliant at working out everyone else's faults. And I was the one who wanted to be an artist, someone who was supposed to see things with a clear unbiased eye! I'd been blind to anything good in Brian, only seeing what I wanted to. I thought about what he'd said about Carl Niemenen. He was right. It *did* take courage to do what he was doing. I wondered if Peter would see it that way. Maybe things might change between them, now that Peter knew his father had left him behind because he didn't want him hurt.

Feet clicked and clattered up and down the corridor outside. Two female voices laughed over something and faded. The curtain at the window rose and fell gently with the wind's breath.

If things were going to change in *our* home, *I'd* have to change. Not what I believed, but the way I looked at people. I'd have to see things from their side. Was that what loving them meant? Accepting people without trying to shape them into what suited me?

Then it dawned on me that really that was the way God did it. He accepted us first. He'd loved me before I ever thought about him. I hadn't had to change and be good before he could begin loving me. And Jesus hadn't died on the cross for me because I was nice to know. He'd done it out of pure love.

I closed my eyes and prayed again for Brian and Mum, that God would show me, more and more, how to love them. And that some day, somehow, they'd know his love for them too.

I think I dozed for a few minutes, for I jerked when the door opened.

"Hello. I've been sent on ahead with emergency rations."

"Neil! How on earth did you get in? Did the nurse see you?"

"Your Dad twisted her arm a wee bit. This isn't much but it's all we could find. Roddy and Peter are trying the canteen."

I took the paper bag and looked inside. Digestive biscuits, two bars of chocolate and some green seedless grapes.

"They're Karen's. We've been camping out in her private room."

"Poor Karen."

"Save your sympathy. She's having a great time. She's crushed us all at draughts, and had three chapters of *The Wind in the Willows* read to her. Peter's got no voice left."

"Peter's been reading to her?"

"Did you think he was illiterate?"

I looked down at the bed cover. Neil had a terrific knack of making me feel like a heel. My brain had decided to stop judging people, but my big mouth hadn't got the message yet. I took a chocolate bar out and began to unwrap it.

"I've been thinking about what to get you for Christmas. Of course, I'll need to know what size you take," he announced.

I stopped in mid bite.

"Neil, if this is one of your . . ."

"The hospital might know of a suppliers somewhere."

"For what?"

"The strait-jacket I'm going to get you."

"Very funny."

I lay back on the pillow and closed my eyes. Wishing he'd go away. When I opened them, he was sitting on the chair Larry had used earlier.

"Sorry," he said.

I stared resolutely at the cover.

"How's the leg?"

"Sore."

He rested his chin on his folded arms on the back of the chair. His eyes were a darker brown than Larry's. I couldn't read them at all.

"I meant I was sorry I left you. At the garage."

He was watching me carefully.

"Remember when we were in his office? I saw a Merc being moved into one of the sheds. The same colour as your Dad's. I wanted to make sure. But I should have stayed with you. It was stupid . . ."

"Was it his?"

"They'd taken the plates off, but it was the right model. I was only gone a couple of minutes. I went out to the street, but you'd vanished into thin air."

"What did you do?"

"I went back to the receptionist. Delaney was with her. But neither of them had seen you, so I wandered up the street for a while, then I reckoned something was wrong, so I found a police station."

I held out two squares of nut chocolate. A peace offering. He took them, then he sat up.

"I'd better go and see if they've found any food."

"Don't you dare," I protested. "Not till you tell me everything that happened. It's awful just having to lie here."

"Well," he began, "I waited in the police station for a while, then this big guy with a black beard appeared. I didn't realize who he was, not right away. He fired questions at me. I couldn't understand how he knew so much, till it dawned on me he was Larry.

"He left at top speed, and a policeman brought me here. Roddy and Peter were here already with his sister. She's a nice wee thing. What's the matter? Is it your leg?"

"No. I had a tetanus shot." I moved carefully off the tender area. "So how did Larry find us?"

"Because of the car. Your dad's car, that is. The police were already interested in Mr Delaney's business activities. They'd an open file on those two men who were holding you. They knew where to find them, but somebody had warned them. I mean, warned the crooks. Brian thinks it might have been Delaney himself. Anyway, the police were already following you when you ran into the demonstration . . ."

He broke off as the door opened. Peter and Roddy came in on tiptoe, looking for all the world like a pair of burglars. Peter was carrying a plate with a metal lid over it.

"Sausage and egg," he said. "All they had." Roddy produced a knife and fork, and sat on the end of the bed. Peter squatted on the floor. I lifted the plate lid, then saw that they were all watching me.

"You're not going to stay and watch me eat it?" I said helplessly. They looked at one another.

"We risked life and limb to bring it to you," Roddy said. "We had to grovel at the canteen."

"Not to mention creeping practically on all fours past the sister's desk," Peter added.

I looked at them, and the sausages and the egg, and laid down the fork.

"Actually, I'm not all that hungry."

"I told you she was thrawn," Neil said at once to Peter. "She never knows what she wants, till you tell her she can't have it."

Peter grinned, Roddy smiled and Neil was looking smug. I couldn't decide which one to throw the plate at.

The door opened and the doctor who'd sewn me up earlier came in.

"Hey, too many bodies in here," he protested mildly.

"Just leaving," Roddy said quickly.

"See you later," Peter added, and the three of them made a hasty exit.

Then I had to lie back and try to be calm, while

the doctor pumped up a black thing round my arm, checked my blood pressure and took my pulse. Calm was the last word to describe how I was feeling, but to my relief he announced, "Well, everything's normal. I think you'll live."

"You mean I'm all right? I can go home?"

"I think so. We'll get a chair to take you to the door. Keep your weight off the leg for a few days. Plenty of rest."

After he'd gone, nothing happened for what seemed like ages. I grew more and more frustrated, expecting every minute that someone would appear with the promised wheelchair. When the door finally opened, it was only Peter.

"I'm a spy," he said hurriedly. "If that fierce woman sees me, I'm done for." He came right in, closing the door behind him. "What did the doctor say?"

"Everything's OK," I told him.

"Good."

Then he leaned back against the wall, with his hands thrust in his pockets, and stared at the floor. He looked deflated, and I wondered why. I thought about how rotten I'd been to him. Immersed in my own misery, I hadn't had any time for his.

He looked up.

"I just had a word or two with the old man."

At first I thought he meant Brian, then I realized he meant he'd spoken to his father in America.

"And?"

He made a face.

"I understood most of what he said. Luckily it wasn't a very good line."

"Was he really angry?"

"Absolutely livid," he said slowly, separating all the syllables.

"He should have taken you with him," I said after a moment or two.

"Oh, sure. What difference would that have made? He'd have kept me locked up in hotel rooms."

"He doesn't want you to get hurt."

Peter stared at his feet again. He looked unconvinced.

"Well, anyway," I began jokily, "if you had gone, you wouldn't have met your fantastic new neighbours."

He didn't react.

"Or their totally amazing friends from north of the border," I added, a little desperately.

"Amazing's not the word," he said, without looking up. "They're being so nice to me, I don't know how much more of it I can take."

He's angry at himself, I thought. He was doing all right until he spoke to his father. Now he feels he's made a fool of himself, and he's angry. I couldn't bear to see him looking so miserable, and I said the first thing that came into my head.

"Peter, if Mum doesn't want to paint your horse, I could do it. Not in oils," I went on, "but I'm pretty good with pastels. And you'd save money. She charges quite a lot . . ."

He smiled faintly.

"But you'd have to tie it up," I began. Then the door opened yet again. This time it was Neil.

"See you later," Peter said abruptly, and he was gone before Neil could speak or stop him.

"I didn't know he was here," Neil said awkwardly.

"He just came to find out what the doctor said."

"Oh, right. So did I. What did he say?"

"I can go home. I'm normal."

Neil muttered something in Gaelic.

"Do you have to?" I said tiredly. "I hate it when you two speak in Gaelic."

"If it upsets you so much, you should learn it."

"In about a million years."

"Even you wouldn't take that long. We could give you a few lessons next week."

"Next week I'm in Cornwall."

"No, you're not. Brian has to stay around till everything's settled with the police. Maybe the week after, he said. Your house is going to be bulging at the seams by the time your Mum comes back. Campbells in every corner. We're thinking of teaching Peter to fish," he added.

I tried to imagine Peter sitting placidly on the river bank with a rod and line. It wasn't easy.

"Does Larry know?"

"He said it sounded like a good idea. He'll keep an eye on us."

We both fell silent. I guessed that Neil's thoughts were much the same as mine. I hoped fervently that Larry was right, and that the men who had tried to blackmail Mr Niemenen had no real intention of carrying out their threats. Perhaps they would soon be caught. But, even if we didn't know what was going to happen, we couldn't abandon Peter now.

When Neil spoke next, I sensed he was trying to distract me. "You know, I couldn't believe it when Peter said he didn't even have a rod. With all that river in his own garden. Isn't it incredible?"

"Incredible," I agreed.

"You could always sit on the bank and watch us. Rest your leg."

"So I could."

"Paint some pictures of us."

I looked at his head, seeing his ears for the first time.

They were very neat. In my mind, I took an imaginary pencil round the line of his jaw. I liked the shape of that too.

"I was really worried about you," he said quietly.

"Were you?"

"Mmm."

A happy feeling began spreading through me. I wondered why I'd ever thought he wasn't good-looking. And the way he was looking at me somehow made me feel as if I wanted to dance round the room.

"Really worried?"

"Uhuh."

"Why?"

He said something else in Gaelic.

"What did you say? Was that an insult?"

He laughed and he wouldn't tell me. But it hadn't sounded like an insult. He wouldn't say any more except, "See you later."

When he'd gone I lay back against the pillows, thinking about going home and the week ahead. There was nothing else for it. As soon as I could, I'd have to get hold of a Gaelic phrase-book or something. Renoir would have to wait.